OHIO
DOMINICAN
UNIVERSITY™
SINCE 1911

The Last Codfish

The Last Codfish

J. D. McNeill

Henry Holt and Company
New York

With thanks to Jessie Haas, Mike Daley, and the Monday night writers' group for their support and encouragement.
To Christy Ottaviano for her vision and guidance.
To June Field Darling for being a mentor on so many levels.
To my husband for his love, strength, and faith.

Henry Holt and Company, LLC
Publishers since 1866
115 West 18th Street
New York, New York 10011
www.henryholt.com

Henry Holt is a registered trademark of Henry Holt and Company, LLC

Distributed in Canada by H. B. Fenn and Company Ltd.

Library of Congress Cataloging-in-Publication Data
McNeill, J. D.
The last codfish / by J. D. McNeill.—1st ed.
p. cm.
Summary: Fifteen-year-old Tut lives in squalor with his fisherman father on the coast of Maine, but his English teacher and a new neighbor girl are determined to turn his life around and force him to speak, which he has not done since his mother's death.
ISBN-13: 978-0-8050-7489-9
ISBN-10: 0-8050-7489-9
[1. Mutism, Elective—Fiction. 2. Single-parent families—Fiction. 3. Friendship—Fiction. 4. Teachers—Fiction. 5. Grief—Fiction. 6. Fishing—Fiction. 7. Maine—Fiction.] I. Title.
PZ7.M4787953Las 2005 [Fic]—dc22 2004054025

First Edition—2005
Design by Patrick Collins
Printed in the United States of America on acid-free paper. ∞
1 3 5 7 9 10 8 6 4 2

In memory of Ben and Josh

Dedicated to Kristina, Paige, and James

The Last Codfish

ONE

THE END OF JULY.

TUT ROLLED THE NOTE into a thin tube and stuffed it inside the wine bottle. Then pounded in the cork with the palm of his hand. He was alone on the wide rock at the end of Sutter's Point. The wind came off the ocean hard and cold, roaring in his ears, drowning the sounds of the waves below. He turned like a discus thrower. When he neared the edge of the rock, he let go of the bottle. It seemed to hang for just a moment at the highest point of the arc and then fell, dark and sparkling, into the gray water.

The tide was going out. Most of the fishermen had already come in. But there was still no sign of his father's boat. The worry of it gnawed at his insides.

Tut shaded his eyes with his hand, trying hard to see what wasn't there. Mr. White had told him once that worrying didn't do a lick of good. But right now worry seemed to be the best-possible option to Tut. It prepared him for what might be hiding, just out of sight.

"Hi!" a girl's voice came from behind him. It was the new girl who had moved into town a few weeks ago. She was dressed in thick-soled sneakers, jeans, and an oversized sweatshirt. Tut's grandmother, Esta, would have taken one look at her and said, "She's from *away.*"

"My name is Alex," she said, holding out her hand to him. He had no idea what to do with that, so he turned back to the sea. The water was the same color as Alex's eyes. Her hair was like the dark seaweed that floated in the waves. Tut bit his lower lip. The taste of salt reminded him of how hungry he was.

"They say you don't talk," Alex said, sitting down beside him. "Is it because you can't or because you won't?"

Tut wished there was some way to jump off Sutter's Point without breaking both legs.

"I love to talk. People are always telling me I talk too much. When I heard that you hadn't said a word in years, I thought maybe we could be friends. If I love to talk and you can't, what could be more perfect than that?"

Death by fire ants? was the first thing that came to Tut's mind. He kept his hands still, resisting the urge to sign the words. Across the channel a wide band of wet stones showed how low the tide was getting. In another hour the channel would be too shallow for a boat the size of his father's to come in safely. The current beyond the islands would be roaring now. If his father came up from the south, he'd be okay. . . . Every once in a while his father stayed out all night. Tut never knew when one of those nights would be.

"How did you lose your voice?" Alex's words drew him back. "Our landlord said you talked when you were little. Here," she said, and held out a pad of paper and a stubby pencil. "I always carry paper with me. I hate it when I think of words that are just right and later when I try to remember them, they're lost. If you write, then we'll be able to communicate."

Tut hadn't spoken since his mother died. From that moment words stopped for him and he couldn't seem to get them started again. He'd learned to trust silence.

He looked out again to the open sea. That was what he was used to, the sounds of sea and wind, and waiting for his father to come home. There was a small gray dot coming from the south. He willed it to be his dad. Alex's arm brushed his. He didn't want to, but he looked at her. The wind blew her hair back from her face and she smiled into it.

"What are you looking for?" she asked. Their eyes locked until Tut couldn't stand it anymore. He looked back out. It was his father's boat. He started running toward the harbor. It felt good to be moving away from her, up the thin trail of sand that cut through the heavy sea grass. He ran hard, all the time hoping she wasn't behind him. One more dash and he was up over the side of the bank and the harbor spread out in front of him like a painting.

The long pier stood high above the low water. Gulls flew in loose circles above the boats. The flash of red and orange, yellow and green, on the different boats brought names to Tut's mind. The MacGregors, Wheelers, Nathan Briggs, and the others. Tut thought of their faces as he emptied the sand from his shoes.

Over the roof of the fish market he could see the white shape of the *Merry Anna II* coming in much too fast. Her wake made the moored boats bob up and down against their ropes. Tut worried that they'd break. Someday the harbormaster would fine him. Tut knew the man turned his back out of pity. Everyone pitied Winston Tuttle, especially Winston Tuttle himself.

Tut ran quickly over the gravel parking lot. His feet sounded like a drum on the gray dock boards. The boat's motor shifted to reverse to slow her down. The engine was cut and she glided silently up to the side of the dock. His father threw Tut the bow line without a word. He caught it and tied it secure. He tied the stern line too, then jumped down onto the deck to help with the catch. The air smelled of exhaust, fish, and whiskey.

"Did ya ever see such a pitiful catch in yer life, Tut?" his father moaned as Tut pulled the fish from the hold. "Look at that scrawny bluefish. Whose going ta buy that? And that codfish, Tut, it's the size of a sardine, fer cryin' out loud! Who in hell's going to want a cod like that?" His father's black hair curled around the edges of his hat. His wide shoulders filled the jacket he wore, but the bottom of it hung loose. He didn't eat right and Tut worried about that too.

Tut had to get the fish to the market. He used the crane to lift it up onto the dock, then pushed it over the worn planks. The boat's motor droned as it moved to the mooring. Tut hoped his dad would be careful.

"Kept open just for you, Tut," Mr. White bellowed from the far end of the building. He walked like he was moving down the rolling deck of a ship instead of the flat wooden floor. "Why, look at that," he said. "You know I haven't seen a decent cod in three weeks. This one here's perfect eatin' size."

Tut watched the man's big hands. Mr. White put his

finger on the scale so that the fish weighed more. Tut's face burned with shame. He knew that Mr. White did that often. When he was done weighing the fish, he gave a handful of bills to Tut.

It amazed Tut how his father could hardly walk but could jump from the big boat into the skiff night after night and not fall into the sea and drown. When he got to shore, he threw his arm over Tut's shoulders and they headed for the marsh path. Tut saw Mr. White turn off the lights in the market, then stand in the dark door, watching them as they walked past.

Two

THEY HAD WORN the path on the edge of the marsh wide enough so they could walk side by side. A mist was beginning to blow in from the sea. Before long it would be the kind of fog that makes you feel blind. At the far end of the marsh Tut led his dad up a rocky bank and onto the road. His father's eyes were almost shut, his lips formed a straight line across his unshaven face.

"It's changing, Tut. Everything's changing," he muttered as they cut through an abandoned lot. They stepped through a break in a bed of wild beach roses and were on their street. Tut looked up at the sign. Norman Wheeler told him once that every capital city in America had insane asylums built on streets named Pleasant Street. Tut didn't doubt it.

When they got to his house, Tut pulled open the door of the long, narrow shed. The air smelled old and musty. Tut's father stumbled on the kitchen step. He landed on his side on the floor and didn't move to get up.

"Someday there ain't going to be any more codfish, Tut," he sobbed. "Someday some stupid son of a bitch is going to catch the last one and there won't be no more cod, ever again." His eyes closed. Tut knelt beside him until his thin cheeks puffed out and pulled in with steady rhythm. He'd sleep through the night. Tut covered him with a blanket, then went outside to sit on the back steps.

He looked up the hill at the Shaws' place. It was the first house on the road that rose above the marsh behind Tut's. Alexis Carlson was Alex's real name. She and her mother were renting the Shaws' house for the year. Tut dreaded them being so close. Most people didn't talk much when they were around Tut. If they did, they hardly ever talked to him. No one except Mr. White or Widow Banks had spoken to him the way Alex had.

Tut thought about Alex's question, "Can't talk or won't?" He didn't know the answer. All he knew was that when he tried to speak, he got scared. Not just a little frightened, but more like horrified. The same feeling he got when he stayed in a boat too long. When the speech therapist had seen how upset he got, she'd stopped making him try. Instead she'd taught him to speak with his hands. His father had learned just enough sign language to get by. Tut took a deep breath. He opened his mouth, but no sound came. His breathing was coming harder now and he felt like he was choking, but he forced himself to do it again. Suddenly all the horrible sensations of that one awful moment filled him; there were explosions and fire that seemed so real. He was on his feet running as hard as he could to get away.

Headlights came out of nowhere and Tut ran for the ditch. He stumbled and fell. Pain ripped through his knee. He rolled to his feet and was running again.

"Are you all right?" a woman's voice called after him in the dark. He ran on.

"Tut!" he heard Alex yell.

He ran until he came to Sutter's Point, where he fell flat on the big stone, buried his head in his arms, and sobbed until it went away. He rolled onto his back and looked up into the sky. The black form of the twisted pine rose up at the edge of the stone. Exhausted, he crawled to the tree and dug into the sand by its roots, pulled the tall grasses down around himself, and tried to sleep.

Hours later, Tut woke to gulls circling above, their forms drifting in and out of the gray mist. They sounded like rusty hinges. *Sky rats!* he thought as he pulled himself to his feet and headed toward town. Ghostlike shapes of the fishing boats floated out into the bay. He had to get home and wake up his father. Every morning he made sure that his dad was on the boat by five. They hadn't talked about it being Tut's job, it just was.

He wished he hadn't run so far. With his knee hurting badly, it would be faster walking through town on the flat surface than through the marsh. The streets were practically silent. The dark shapes of each building came out of the mist. He knew them all so well. Wendy Pride's Café had the best cinnamon buns north of Boston. It said so right on the sign. The smell of coffee mingled with bacon and fresh-baked bread. He'd give anything for just a bite.

He wasn't expecting the headlights that cut through the mist. It was Mr. White's old blue pickup. Tut tried to hide in the shadows between Baker's store and the bank. But the brakes squealed on the ancient truck.

"What in blazes happened to you?" Mr. White slammed the door shut and headed toward him. "You been out all night?"

Tut didn't move.

"Looks like you skinned yer knee clean off." Mr. White squatted down to get a better look. "You get your butt in my truck," he ordered. "That there needs stitches."

The last time Tut had gone to the clinic, the police had come to his house and talked to his dad. When they'd left, his dad was quiet for days. Then he was sorry. Then, it seemed to Tut, he just drifted farther away. Tut shook his head.

Mr. White sighed. "Okay, okay, I won't take you to the clinic," he said, softer. "At least let me give you a ride home."

Tut nodded. That would be okay. Mr. White helped him into the truck.

"You wait here. I got to see Baker a minute." Tut watched as he pounded on the door of the dark store.

"I know yer in there, you old mouse. Open up," he yelled.

The door slowly opened and Mr. White disappeared inside. Tut's gaze traveled to the houses that continued up the hill. The lit windows made pale lights in all the mist. The Flynns, Hoopers, McCoys, and Wilsons, generations of fishermen.

His knee throbbed and he began to feel restless. Just as he was thinking about getting out of the truck, the door to the store opened and Mr. White stepped out. He set a bag on the seat next to Tut. He tried not to look but couldn't help it. There were eggs in that bag and bacon and bread. There was a box of doughnuts, the kind that has white powder and cinnamon sugar and plain all in the same box. Like his mother used to buy, years ago.

"When was the last time you ate anything, Tut?" Mr. White asked.

Tut shrugged, then turned and watched the houses that flashed by the window. When was the last time he'd eaten? He really couldn't remember. His stomach ached and he wanted one of those doughnuts. Mr. White shifted up through the gears and down as he drove. When they stopped in front of Tut's house, the windows were dark. His father would still be asleep.

"You take these." Mr. White pushed the groceries toward Tut. Tut shook his head, but it didn't matter. "You take them dad-burned groceries. If you want to work them off, you can come down and clean the market. Will that make it okay?"

Tut nodded, but kept his eyes low.

"In the bottom of that bag, there's some peroxide and bandages. You make sure that knee gets cleaned up good." Tut looked up at the older man and nodded. Mr. White looked madder than hell, but Tut wasn't sure why. The sound of tires grinding on loose stones faded as Tut walked into the dark shed.

He set the bag on the bench, pulled out the box of doughnuts, and ran his finger under the white cardboard. The first doughnut was gone in three bites. He brushed the sugar from his sweatshirt, then draped his winter coat around the bag. His knee was so stiff. The lower leg of his pants was caked with blood and sand. He wished that Mr. White hadn't seen that.

His father was just where he'd left him. His head was back and his mouth open. Tut poked him with his foot and he sat up instantly.

"What time is it?" he yelled.

Tut watched as his father struggled to his feet, then made his way to the sink. He took all of the dishes that were piled there and set them on the already-full counter. He splashed fresh water on his face, then let it run through his hair. He was dressed before he looked at Tut.

"What happened to you?" he asked.

I fell, Tut signed. He wouldn't tell him the whole story. It would be a waste of time.

His father ran a pan of warm water and made Tut take off his ripped pants. His father's hands shook as he cleaned away the dirt. Tut winced as the water brought back the pain. He watched his father's face, tanned like leather. His dark hair was wet, but still thick and curly. It was so different from Tut's own golden hair.

When his father finished, the wound was bleeding

slowly. He put a big wad of gauze over it, then wrapped strips of a torn sheet around that. He stared into Tut's eyes for the first time in days. Tut saw the old look flash across his face. He'd said once that Tut looked so much like his mother, it hurt. Tut knew his father was thinking about this now. That was what made him hurry away and what kept him out on the sea for so long.

Three

Tut held his hand against the glass as his father disappeared into the fog. *He's in a hurry,* thought Tut. *He needs to get out on the water.* Good fishing was getting scarce and competition over good spots was fierce. Auctions of boats and traps were too common. One piece of bad luck could mean having to give up the sea.

Tut knew the worry of it hung over his father's head. He stared at the empty fog for a moment. Back when his mother was alive, she'd stand in the same spot and watch until his father was out of sight.

He pulled on a pair of shorts. His knee throbbed. He took the doughnuts from the shed and went out to the back steps. The doughnuts stood in three rows; only one was missing. He picked a white-powdered one and bit into the sweet sugar.

"Are you all right?" Alex's voice came from the corner of the garden.

Tut looked up and wished instantly that she'd go away.

She sat down beside him on the steps and helped herself to one of the cinnamon-covered doughnuts.

"Gwen almost hit you last night. Are you okay?" she asked again. She had a small pad of paper in her hand.

He moved the doughnuts to the other side of his body.

"Why were you running like that? You looked like you were scared."

He was taking small bites, staring across the marsh, wondering how to get rid of her.

"I won't leave this spot until you tell me."

She sounded so determined, he knew she meant it. What on earth was he going to do with Alex Carlson on his back step all day?

"Well, if you don't write, I'll talk. I won't waste all the words that are in my head. I think that if you don't say things, the words get wasted. Gwen is my mother," she explained, as if Tut cared. "She's the one who almost hit you. She hates being called Mom, so I call her Gwen. She says it makes her feel too old to be called Mom." She munched her doughnut and moved down to sit cross-legged in the grass, facing him.

"Gwen says she needs to find herself. That's why

we're in Maine. She thinks she's an artist now. When I was little, she studied interior decorating in Boston. Have you ever been to Boston?" she asked him. Tut looked away. "Well, she insisted that people's houses should be the color of their 'inner beings.' But nobody liked the color of their inner being very much." Alex eyed the doughnut box. "Anyway, when I was ten, we went to Vermont so she could study cooking. That part was cool. But Gwen believes that wheat bran should be added to everything from scrambled eggs to cheese-cake. So she always ended up as a dishwasher."

Tut picked up his doughnuts and walked into the house. He latched the door. In the kitchen he pulled the old coffeepot out from under the sink. Then he went out to the shed and grabbed the bag of groceries. When he passed the door, he glanced out. She was still there, staring at him through the glass.

He decided to make himself an egg sandwich. If a man knew how to make a decent egg sandwich, he was pretty close to being a chef as far as Tut was concerned. He toasted some of the bread while the bacon fried, then cooked an egg until the yolk was stiff. He piled it all together and wondered if Alex Carlson was still sitting in the grass.

Tut went into the parlor with his food and closed the

door. One more door standing between him and Alex made him feel a little safer.

The parlor had been his mother's room. Tut took her picture from the shelf and put it beside him on the couch. She was laughing; next to her in the boat was a big golden dog that looked as if she was smiling too. *Lady.* The wind was blowing his mother's hair. He remembered her being like the sun and light, where his father seemed to him to be all rain and dark and storm. They were so different. There were things that he remembered clearly, like her eyes and the way they sparkled. He had pictures to remind him. But he couldn't remember the sound of her voice.

He took a bite of the sandwich and then picked up the book he'd started reading the day before. It was a thin book of poetry. Tut had tried to read every book in her library at least once, as if by reading the books, he might find answers to questions he'd lost the power to ask.

There was a pounding at the door. Alex was probably getting really ticked off by now. He stayed right where he was and ate his sandwich. After a while the pounding stopped.

Tut finally fell asleep and dreamed of his mother. She was standing in the back of the boat and turned to him with a smile. He threw his arms around her waist. But when he looked inside the circle of his arms, nobody was there. He woke, shaken. He hated to dream of her. The bad dreams were awful. The good dreams were never enough.

FOUR

THE FIRST OF AUGUST.

SATURDAY MORNING Tut peeked cautiously out the kitchen window. The last few days, it seemed like every time he'd walked out of his house, Alex was waiting for him. He searched every corner of the yard, the long broken fence by the garden, the thin trunks of the lilac bushes, the empty clothesline.

Tut was used to being able to come and go freely. He'd never had to worry about anyone hanging around. No one had ever walked into his yard before by accident. Why would a girl like Alex *want* to be there? There were so many other kids in school, why would she pick him to be a friend? Tut took comfort in the fact that soon she would probably lose interest and go away.

Tut worked for Widow Banks every Saturday afternoon because she made the best spaghetti sauce in the whole village. It was thick with sausages and meatballs and seasoned with garlic, fresh basil, and cheese. If Tut weeded her gardens and mowed her lawn, she'd give him a plate heaped high with homemade noodles and sauce.

Tut opened the door and stepped out cautiously. Black-eyed Susans bloomed in deep yellow masses at the edge of their yard. The fireweed's tall purple spikes grew beside them. Tut took out his pocketknife and started to rip through the stems of the flowers as quickly as he could. Widow Banks loved flowers. He wiped the knife blade on his shorts.

His knee was still a little stiff. He walked as fast as he could to the next corner. The air was growing warmer and Tut was beginning to relax when he heard the sound of feet on pavement. He spun around to see Miss Berry, the new English teacher, jogging toward him.

He was two streets away from Widow Banks's house and right beside him was a huge bed of wild roses. He wanted to dive into those bushes, but the thorns stopped him. He stood helplessly visible and watched as she turned just one street away and headed out the road that followed the shore. She hadn't seen him.

She'd been a substitute teacher toward the end of last year. But this year she would be his English teacher. He'd made a mistake with her. She'd asked for an essay and he'd written a poem. Usually teachers just figured he'd copied some poet, gave him a mediocre grade, and that was it. It had always worked for Tut before, but she wrote, *Wonderful use of language.* He'd caught her looking at him as if she was weighing something in her mind. He was desperate to know what she was thinking. What would happen when he had her every day?

Tut started up a slight rise past a row of gray-shingled cottages. When he reached the top, he could see the widow. Her hair was twisted into a heavy bun, her apron was blowing about in the breeze. A mass of gray-and-white gulls paced the lawn around her, demanding a treat, while others were suspended in the breeze, screeching for her to feed them.

There were two things that Tut didn't like about the widow. First, she talked far too much. She called him "you poor boy," and Tut hated that. She had no way of knowing how it made him feel. Tut knew that she meant well, so he tried to let it go. The other thing that he hated was her love for the gulls. To him their calls sounded like a door creaking, an awful rusty hinge that was forced to open and shut. Then sometimes it sounded like they were laughing, and he hated that even more. She always made an extra loaf of bread for them and fed them all the scraps from her table. Tut would have given anything for those scraps. She was smiling up into their greedy yellow eyes and he wondered what she saw that he didn't. She threw them the last of the bread and then looked his way.

"Tut, what lovely flowers!" she cried.

He opened the gate as the last of the gulls flew away and handed her the bouquet.

"I wonder what it would be like to be a bird, so free, so wild." She looked fondly after the gulls. "Come, come, I have to show you what you did for me last week! What's happened." Tut followed her to the backyard. Tut had pruned a rosebush that had been choked by the honeysuckle around it. He'd spent hours cutting back the stalks, then pruning the thorny, dead branches off the rose. Now there were tiny new leaves all over the plant.

"It will bloom good next summer," she said. "I'll show you what to do today." They walked to the fence that stood near the road. "See the weeds in there? I'll want to dig up these plants for the greenhouse next month, so those weeds have to go."

Tut sat down on the ground and started working. The widow leaned against the top rail of the fence, talking about every single thing that had happened since last Saturday. Tut just tuned her out. He had memorized poems from his mother's books and while the widow told him about her cousin Helen's gallstones and her fisherman son's arthritis, Tut went over the words of the poems. As he pulled pigweed away from the base of her huge oregano plant, words poured through his mind. *When I was a child, I walked through wheat. And it beat the sky above my head. Though alone I was not afraid, the contour of the land the same, as winter snow or short spring grass. I knew the land and was not afraid.* The scent of the herbs and the words blended together for Tut.

"Can I help?" Alex's voice came from behind him, tearing through the rhythms of the words.

Tut shook his head vehemently. No one was going to share his sauce with him, especially her.

"Why, of course you can, dear." Widow Banks smiled over the fence at Alex. "Who are you? I can't say as I've seen you around."

"I'm Alexis. We're living up at the Shaws' house," Alex told her.

"Roberta's dream home. She wanted so badly to live in a place where she could see the ocean. Poor dear, died before they could move in. You two are neighbors, then. Do you know Tut?"

"We've met," Alex said.

Tut could feel the color shoot up his neck and into his cheeks. He just leaned closer to his work and pulled weeds out from under the basil.

"He's a good boy, that one," Widow Banks said.

"He seems very nice." Tut could tell that Alex was looking at him, and he wasn't going to give her the satisfaction of looking up. "But he's not very friendly," she added.

"Oh, he's a loner, just like his father."

Tut could feel the heat rise inside himself.

"Do you like to cook?" the widow asked.

"I think I'd love to, but I don't know how," Alex said.

"The problem with the world today is that no one takes the time to teach young people to cook. They grow up not knowing what flour is. All you do is open a box and throw in an egg and oil, and there you are. So many girls never learn how to boil water, much less make decent pasta. You want to learn?" Alex nodded. "If I teach you how to make my pasta, I guarantee Tut will be your best friend for life. Won't you, Tut?"

The two of them walked to the house, the old woman with her hair twisted into her tight bun and Alex's free and wild. Tut watched until the door closed behind them. He weeded the rest of the section and brooded. Homemade pasta wasn't the answer to all the freaking problems in the world, but oh, how he wanted a bowl of it.

Tut raked the weeds and took them to the compost pile, all the time wondering what to do. Should he go to the house? Widow Banks would make him wash with hot water and soap. She'd insist that he use the brush to get the dirt out from under his nails. Then she'd make him sit across from Alex and eat. He hadn't had any breakfast. He walked quietly to the porch and looked in the window.

Alex was standing next to the table, running thin strips of dough through the cutter. She chattered almost constantly. Tut sat down under the window and listened.

"What makes garlic smell so good?" Alex asked. "Why are there so many different kinds of olive oil? Why did you use fresh tomatoes when the canned sauce is so easy?" But then she asked, "Can Tut write? I keep trying to get him to write, but he won't."

"I guess he can write. He has a book he carries with him where he writes down things. He let me see a poem he'd written once. He writes beautiful poetry."

As her words poured out the window, Tut could feel a ripping inside himself. He wanted to make her shut up. He'd brought his journal with him once and the widow had found it while he worked. He'd come back and she was reading it. He'd grabbed it out of her hands. It had been three weeks before her sauce had lured him back into her yard. He did not want Alex to know that he was able to spell the word *cat,* much less write poems.

Tut crawled off the porch, then walked away as fast as he could.

FIVE

When tut got home, he searched through the trash for just the right bottle and found a thin amber one. There was a tiny bit of wine left inside and he poured it out in the grass beside the shed door, then blew in the bottle to dry it. Tut hated the smell—yeasty and sweet. He set it on the step in the sun, then walked into his mother's parlor and pulled a piece of paper from the drawer and wrote,

Mom,

I have a problem. This girl Alex seems to be everywhere. It's as if she's following me. She bothers me and I hate that she bothers me. I don't know what to do with her. Most people just go away, but she doesn't. How can I get rid of her?

Love, Tut

He folded the note, grabbed the bottle on his way out, stuffed both in his backpack, and started off toward Sutter's Point.

Tut searched the roads and lawns for some sign of Alex. She should still be back at the widow's house. The old woman didn't let people get away that easily. Nope. He was sure that Alex would still be there, stuffing down his meatballs.

The tide was in and the water was close to the path. The marsh looked like a huge lake at high tide. When it went out, there would be islands of grass cut through with deep channels. He moved slowly along the path and across the harbor road. The afternoon sun warmed him.

He stopped on the big rock and let his backpack fall to the ground. Waves were pounding along the shore. Tut took the bottle from his pack and slipped the note in. The words showed through the glass. He swung his arm and let the bottle fly into the air.

He wanted to be out on the water today. Every once in a while, when he and his father were together on the boat, there was something between them that was magic. The way his father smiled at him for catching a fish. The boat was one of the few places where Tut's silence didn't matter. Tut turned and started slowly back toward the harbor.

The wind blew in gusts, making the sea grass move first one way and then another. Mr. White said once, "The sea was here long before we were born and will be here long after we're gone." It was hard for Tut to imagine wind and water being so much stronger than flesh and blood. It seemed to him that people meant too much to be so fragile.

At the edge of town he came face-to-face with Norman Wheeler and his friend, Jason Blare.

"Hey, stupid," Norman said, blocking Tut's way with his bike. His short dark hair grew in a point down low on his forehead.

Tut just stood and looked at Norman. To Tut, Norman was like the horseflies that bred in the marshes, simply annoying. Tut stepped to the side. Norman blocked his way again.

"Where'd ya get them nifty clothes? The Salvation Army?"

Tut looked steadily into Norman's eyes. The only thing that Tut was really afraid of, besides talking, was this feeling deep inside. If he let go, if he ever really let go, he wasn't sure what he might do. He knew that if Norman didn't stop, he could hurt him.

Norman took a step back. It was as if he could read Tut's mind.

"Let's go. My ma's waiting," he said to Jason. "So long, stupid," he yelled as he rode off.

Tut stood watching until they disappeared around the corner. It seemed as if the whole world was out to spoil this day. He walked to the fish market, kicking stones and making the sand fly. If he wasn't going to get to eat spaghetti, he could pay back the groceries.

Mr. White looked up from behind the counter. His dark brown eyes shone over the top of his half glasses.

"Howdy, Tut. How's that knee?"

Tut nodded.

"Looks as if it's still attached. That's a good sign. You finally come to pay back them doughnuts? Well, you know where the broom is. Just sweep down the floors and then wash them. Oh, hell, I don't have to tell you what to do."

Tut nodded again and walked to the storeroom. On the floor, beside the broom and dustpan, was a new pair of boots. They were brown and olive green. He picked one up. The inside was soft and cushioned. He had dreamed of wearing boots like that. It smelled brand-new. He put it back down and started to sweep, wondering what they were doing there.

After an hour of sweeping dirt out of every corner in the old market, Tut heard Mr. White talking to someone at the counter.

"Tut! Hey, Tut! You ain't going to believe this!" Mr. White called to him.

Tut leaned the broom against the wall and walked to the front of the store. There was a stranger. A tall man in paint-smeared jeans. His dark hair was pulled back in a ponytail and hung halfway to his hips.

He's from away, Tut thought, and for a moment he wondered why Mr. White had called him. Then he saw the dog.

"Look, Tut! Ain't this dog the spittin' image of your Lady?"

Tut looked into the warm eyes of the golden retriever. She had a wide nose and a square block head. Her coat was a light honey color. Tut took a step closer. The dog, who had been standing quietly, looked at him intently. Her tail started to move. Tut felt as if fireworks were going off inside his head and chest. He knew it couldn't be her, but it looked just like her.

"Have you ever seen a dog that looks more like Lady? She's even the same size. I'd swear that this were one of old Lady's pups. Tut and his mother used to raise these dogs," Mr. White explained to the man. He kept on talking, but Tut didn't hear.

Tut leaned down and the dog came to him. He reached out his hands and touched the fur as she licked his face. He looked into her eyes. No, this wasn't Lady.

He looked up at Mr. White and tears blurred the old man's image. He wrapped his arms around the big golden dog. The smell of her fur, the warmth of her body, it was all so familiar. Tut felt as if he was being pulled through time.

"Well, I'll be damned," Mr. White said. "It's all right, Tut. It's all right, son." He patted Tut's back.

Images flooded Tut's mind. His father had secured Tut's life preserver and thrown him into the cold water. He was floating in the ocean, held above the swells. He could see the boat, the old *Merry Anna.* His father was at the front of the boat. He had thrown a life preserver to Tut's mother and she was about to put it on when Tut yelled for Lady. Lady was still on the boat. He could see his mother reach for the dog seconds before the explosion. When it hit, his father was thrown clear. Tut saw the fire grow and reach up toward the sky. Water came in a rush over him, blinding him as he fought to see. When he got the water out of his eyes, pieces of the boat were raining down around him. After the awful roar, there was an even more horrible silence. A stillness broken only by the hideous laughter of the gulls.

What if he'd shut up? What if he had just shut up?

Six

TUT HELD ON TO the thick golden fur. It was full of the smells of sand and sea, thick with the comforting scent of dog. She smelled like Lady. He inhaled deeply, so ashamed of the tears that wouldn't stop. Mr. White was kneeling beside him on the floor.

"Your dog looked like Willow?" the stranger asked, bending down beside them.

Tut wiped his face quickly on his sleeve and nodded. He took a deep breath, fighting to hold it in.

"I'm sorry, Tut. I wasn't thinking," Mr. White said, still rubbing Tut's back. "He and Lady were together all the time," he explained to the man. "You never saw one of 'em without the other. Tut here even won ribbons at the fair fer dog trainin'. His mother used to brag that he was a better trainer than she was. And she was damn good."

"I haven't trained Willow much," the man said. "I've

never been very good at it. If I was to be truthful, she's done most of the training."

Tut rubbed her chest, the spot just below her collar. The big dog leaned hard against him.

As far as Tut was concerned, this had been one miserable, rotten day from the beginning. He wondered what else could possibly go wrong. Then Tut remembered what Mr. White had said once: "Never ask, What else can go wrong? Cuz it will." He wanted to take back those words, but they'd spilled in his mind like water on sand.

Tut signaled that he wanted to get back to work. Mr. White meant well. Tut knew that, but he also knew what the old man was going to say before he said it. And too many times, he said far too much.

Tut had started to sweep when he became aware that Willow had followed him. He motioned for her to go back, swinging his hand in front of her face. But she didn't go. She sat down right where he was going to sweep. He tried to push her out of the way with the broom, but she pounced her chest down on the floor, her butt in the air, front legs spread. It was an invitation to play. How was he going to be able to ignore that? Maybe he could enjoy her just this one time.

Tut reached up to the shelf where Mr. White kept his stash of crackers. He snapped his fingers and Willow was in front of him. He held a cracker in his hand and motioned to her to sit. He held her collar as he gently pushed her bottom down on the ground. Willow sat. He gave her the cracker and then rubbed her neck vigorously.

Suddenly he became aware of the man's voice. "He seems like such a good kid, but from what the neighbors say, he's so alone. And his disability only adds to that. I'll be honest with you, I'm surprised that no one has done anything about the situation. Their house is a wreck. If things don't improve, surely there will have to be some kind of intervention."

"Don't you believe everything you hear." Mr. White's voice was loud and insistent. "Winston Tuttle ain't a bad man, not really. And damn it, how do ya live through somethin' like that and come out okay? Everyone loved Anna. If someone was hurt, she was there to help. If there was a fire, people would end up stayin' at Tuttle's place"

Tut sat back on his heels and leaned against the wall.

"After it happened, Win fell apart," Mr. White's voice continued. "No one ever thought it would last this long. We all thought he'd come around for the boy's sake, you know? The whole thing is just too all-fired pitiful."

"Well, you know more about it than I do. But where

I come from, people would report something like this to the proper authorities."

Shut up. Tut thought the words as hard as he could.

"I can tell you one thing fer sure. This ain't where you come from. This ain't even close. I guarantee, if the authorities around these parts were called, the only thing that would happen is a bad situation would almost instantly be made one hell of a lot worse."

The man called for Willow and the dog hurried to the door. Tut could see the stranger's face as he glanced quickly back at him. Tut didn't like that the man had seen him cry.

"Well, by Judas priest, I ain't about to open my mouth again today," Mr. White fumed from behind the counter. Tut looked around the corner. The old man grabbed a large fish and slammed it down on the board. "Think you're saying something to make people understand and the next thing you know, everybody's sticking their paw in," he muttered as he cut off the fish's head.

Tut froze as he listened to the jumble of words. He needed to be where he was. What made people think they could muck around in other people's lives anyway? Why did they look at him and think there was something wrong? *Alone,* the man had said. He wondered why that mattered. Wasn't everybody alone, really?

Tut's grandmother used to say it was a shame the way they lived. Whenever she stopped in, she'd go through the house, doing the washing and the dishes, cleaning the floors. All the time she was working, she'd be fussing and scolding Tut. When she left, the house smelled like a strange combination of bleach, lemon, and pine. She and Tut's father had a fight over a year ago. Winston told her to go away. His words had been sharp and biting. Tut had seen the hurt, even on Gramma Esta's hard face.

He wondered what people saw when they looked at his life. Tut remembered the words that had spilled in his mind. *What else could go wrong?* You had to be so careful about what you thought.

SEVEN

WOULD THEY TAKE him away? Tut didn't focus on the floor he was washing, he was so worried about what the stranger had said. Tut knew that things could be better. When his father was really there with Tut, it felt good.

He thought about the man's words, "Their house is a wreck." As he rinsed the floor, those words chewed at him.

Tut put away the bucket. Hanging the mop on its nail, he began to think that he could go home and wash the floors and clean things up. If he made things look better, maybe they'd leave him alone.

He walked past the counter, where Mr. White sat brooding over his record books. When he heard Tut, he turned and looked over the tops of his glasses.

"You done already?" he asked, then paused. "You

know, don't ya, Tut, that if you ever need anything, you can come to me?"

Tut looked into his kind brown eyes and nodded. Yes, he did know that.

"Good." The old man turned back to his books.

Tut was almost out the door.

"Hey, Tut, I almost forgot. Come back here a minute."

Tut wanted to ignore him and just run home, but he stopped and walked back to the counter.

"Them boots out in the back room. I bought them fer my grandson, but they're too small. He's got feet the size of tugboats. He said if he wore them again, he'd be crippled fer life. Be a shame to waste a perfectly good pair of boots. You can take 'em and try 'em. If they don't fit, just throw 'em away."

Tut tried to casually walk back to those shoes. He stuffed them inside his backpack. When he went past the counter, he patted his chest. It was his way of saying thank you.

Mr. White grinned. "You're very welcome."

As Tut rushed home, he thought about Norman's teasing. Tut knew that everyone would wear new clothes on the first day of school. It was the same every year. His father never thought about it, and things like that didn't matter much to Tut either. These new shoes were the kind that the *popular* kids wore. Tut wondered which came first, the popularity or the shoes, and for a minute he almost didn't want to own them.

When he got home, he pulled the shoes out of his bag and set them on the table. The smell of new leather was wonderful. When he tried to put them on, his toes hit something. He reached inside; it was a ball of wadded-up tissue paper. Tut pushed the shoes away and sat looking at them for a long time. Mr. White had bought them for him, not his grandson. He put them on and pulled the laces tight. They were a little big, but nothing a couple pairs of socks couldn't fix.

Tut walked around his house, looking at what needed to be done. He didn't know where to begin. He went outside and stared at the yard. The grass was thigh deep. The lawn mower had broken last summer. There was an old push mower in the shed. Maybe he could use that. The fenced garden was filled with every kind of weed that grows in Maine. He could pull them and start a garden next year, one like the garden Widow Banks had.

He turned to the house. The gray shingles of the cape never looked bad, but the trim was chipped and peeling. That needed painting. The rosebushes around the house were overgrown. He could make it appear like somebody cared. Then he noticed, on the back steps, a pie plate covered with foil, a note taped to the top.

DEAR TUT,

You left without your treat. I hope everything is all right.

I'm sending this along with Alex.

See you next Saturday?

He pulled off the foil and there was a pile of her noodles covered with sauce and a thick sprinkling of cheese. He went into the house, rinsed off a fork, and went back out to sit on the steps. Even cold it tasted good. As he ate, Tut thought about where to begin. The sun was going down. He'd have to wait until tomorrow to start much of anything.

As he watched the shadows grow across the marsh, he wondered why Mr. White and Widow Banks pitied him. He didn't want that. His father detested charity. But the two things that had made this day bearable were the shoes that cushioned his feet and the food that was taking away his hunger.

THE END OF AUGUST.

The last weeks of summer went much too fast. It always felt to Tut that the beginning of school must be similar to a stay in prison, when you know the exact date your captivity begins. He'd spent those days ranging as far and wild as he could over the places that he loved the best.

It seemed to him that Alex had given up. For the past few weeks she hadn't followed him everywhere he went. She didn't show up in his backyard, and she hadn't come to the widow's house the past two Saturdays. But the weird thing was, Tut thought that he should feel better about it than he did.

Sound carries across the marsh far better than most people think. He'd lain awake too many nights and listened to angry voices quarreling. Sometimes the voice was Alex's, but most often it was her mother's. He tried not to listen, but he'd have to be deaf not to hear.

EIGHT

FIRST OF SEPTEMBER.

TUT WOKE to a strong morning light shining in his face. He got out of bed and knelt in front of the screen. The whole eastern rim of the sky was glowing with the dawn. Tut watched until the sun came up full and round. *School starts in a few days,* he thought. He wished the sun would stay right where it was.

The house was silent. Tut dressed quickly and went downstairs. His father was already gone. There was one egg left. Tut fried it with the last of the bacon. Mentally he ran through the list of things that he should do. The list was huge. Tut wished someone would say, "Start right here. Now." He had trimmed the wild roses back into some kind of order and that looked better. What to do next? He had tried the old push mower; it was dull and rusted. Tut was strong, but after an hour he was exhausted and only a small patch of the front lawn was mowed. His plan to get things fixed up hadn't gotten very far.

When he'd finished eating, he went out back to see if there was something he could do to the yard. It was then that he heard the dog barking. At first he couldn't figure out where the sound came from. He ran to the edge of the lawn and looked out over the marsh. The channels were filling with water. Far out in the middle on a quickly shrinking piece of land were a person and a dog.

Tut ran down the hill to the marsh trail, jumping over roots and stones. The tide was coming in fast and Tut knew how cold that water could be. Mr. Nelson kept a boat in the marsh to row out to the clam flats. Tut didn't hesitate but untied the boat and started rowing as fast as he could, following the channel along its curving path. When he got closer, he could hear Alex screaming for help. He pulled the oars with sure strokes.

"Oh, Tut, thank God!" Alex yelled as he came around the last curve in the marsh's channel. He turned and glanced at her. She was up to her knees in the cold water. Willow stood beside her. He'd seen the dog with Alex before. Tut had figured it out. The man that he'd met in the market was her mother's boyfriend. Had to be.

Tut was about to put himself in the position of being

in the same small boat with Alex for a good twenty-minute row. He wondered if God planned stuff like this just to make him miserable.

When he got closer, he could see that Willow's coat was a mass of burrs. She stood in the icy water up to her chest, her mouth open, looking for all the world as if she were smiling.

Tut jumped quickly from the boat, then motioned for Alex to hold it steady.

"Tut, I'm glad to see you!" Alex exclaimed. "It's so early, I was afraid no one would hear us. I thought we'd drown out here." She was shaking as she held on to the side of the boat.

Tut picked up Willow and set her in. It was hard to find a place on her body that wasn't matted with burdock. She jumped to the bottom of the boat. Tut signed to Alex to get in. Moving his hands quickly, emphatically. She seemed puzzled. He pointed to her and then the boat. She understood and climbed over the side while he held it steady. Tut got in and motioned for Willow to stay. All he needed was for the dog to upset the boat and then have to pull them out of the muck and water again.

Tut looked at Willow closely. Nobody with half a brain would let a dog get in that condition.

Perfect idiot, he thought angrily. *It will take hours to comb out her fur. Hours. And all the time she'll be uncomfortable.* Right then he wished he could tell Alex Carlson a thing or two.

Alex sat shivering, and Tut rowed as fast as he could.

"The marsh was beautiful," Alex said after a few minutes. "There were so many things to see. We kept going farther and farther. Willow was having a great time, and I didn't notice that the water was coming in until we were stuck." Her teeth were chattering so much she could hardly talk.

For a time she sat in silence watching him as he rowed.

"You hate me, don't you?" she said.

Hate was a powerful word. He remembered how his mother had disliked it. He stared hard at Alex for a minute and tried to define the feeling he had when he was around her. Tut really didn't want to hate her anymore. But he was mad about Willow. He shrugged and knew that wasn't enough. Tut had gone to a camp about a year after his mother's death, around the time when people figured out that he wasn't going to be talking again. There had been some people there who couldn't hear and he'd watched them read lips.

Wait. He moved his lips to form the word.

Alex nodded as if she understood. She folded her

arms across her knees, rested her head on her arms, and began to cry. Tut wanted to make her stop. He wanted to make her do anything but cry.

Finally she looked up. "Dave's going to kill me when he sees Willow," she said. "He's Gwen's boyfriend. It's his dog. One reason we moved here was so that Mom could be closer to him. He loves Maine. It's the first thing that he and I've agreed on since she met him." Alex pulled her sweatshirt down over her knees. "Gwen hates Maine." She said it so quietly that Tut had a hard time hearing her words. "She's never happy with anything for very long. I love it here. But what I love just doesn't matter much."

Tut could feel something like a wall that he thought was made of stone turning to paper. He rowed the boat to the mooring and jumped gratefully onto solid ground. Alex and Willow followed him to his house. He turned and looked at her, wondering what she wanted.

"You told me to wait," she said.

Tut could see no way around it. He went into his house and got a pencil and piece of paper.

I don't hate you. I just don't know what to do with you, he wrote.

A funny look crossed her face. "Please," she pleaded, "just be my friend."

Nine

TUT FELT THE LAST THREADS of resistance dissolve. He sighed wearily and motioned for her to follow him. They needed to get the burrs out of Willow's coat. It wouldn't take that long if they did it together. In the shed he pushed aside boxes until he found an old, ratty-looking canvas bag in the back corner. His mother had carried it with her to dog shows. When they got that bag out, Lady used to get so excited. It was like she knew that she was going to perform.

"Ya need *all* this stuff?" Alex asked.

Tut looked at the piles of junk and wished it would just go away. He walked past her to the backyard, took two grooming combs from the bag, and handed one to Alex. While Willow sat shaking, they pulled out the burrs. Tut looked into Willow's eyes and knew he could do almost anything to this dog and she'd put up with it.

"My last guidance counselor said that I have control issues," Alex said. "What I'd like to know is, who wouldn't have control issues living with Gwen? I just want to staple her to the wall somewhere. She can't keep running around forever. Do you know what I mean? My goal is to start the school year and end it in the same place at least once before I go to college."

Her fingers were strong as she gently combed Willow's coat.

"Have you always lived here?" she asked.

Tut nodded.

"I'm so jealous. Gwen's threatening to send me to live with my father. I can't remember him. He left two months after I was born. I've seen pictures, but it's like looking at pictures of Prince Charles. I don't have any idea who he is. Gwen says they got along well enough to have me and that was it." Alex shivered. Most of her clothes were still wet.

"You know what I want to be when I grow up? This is going to sound really crazy. I hate school, but I want to be a teacher. If children look at the sky and see it full of oranges and golds and pinks, I want my students not to be satisfied until they know where those colors come from. I want to make people curious. What do you want to be, Tut?"

A fisherman, he wrote. He'd never thought about

there being any other options. For generations, in the Tuttle family, if you were born male, you fished. The boat always went to the oldest son.

"But are you really a fisherman inside?" she asked.

Tut never really cared what was in the net or on the hook. What he loved about being on the water was how the light danced across the surface just before the sun went down, how it made the water look like polished molten gold. It had absolutely nothing to do with fish.

"You know what I *really* want to be?" Alex asked. "A poet. I want to be Shakespeare. Aunt Joanie says that if Shakespeare was alive today, the best he could hope for would be to write obituaries for the *Boston Globe.*"

It was strange for Tut to listen to Alex. He smiled just a little as she rattled away. No one talked to him like she was talking now. Tut worked through the rest of Willow's fur, thinking. He had stacks of journals that he'd filled with words. Most days when he came home from school or sat on Sutter's Point or felt sad, he wrote. He'd sent so many letters out to sea in bottles, it seemed as if the sea must be full of them.

"You know what I want more than anything? I want to find a place that I love and never leave it. And then write poems about it. You've lived here your whole life. Would you ever want to go somewhere else?"

Tut thought of the people that he'd grown up with.

He knew the coast, the woods, the seasons here. Part of him did long to see different places, but he couldn't imagine settling down anywhere else.

He shook his head.

A car drove up the hill. "It's them," Alex said. "I should go see what's happening. Gwen's trying to convince Dave to move in with us. She says the reason he won't is because of me. If he doesn't move in, she wants to go out West. We were headed to New Mexico when they met. She says that the sun shines stronger out there and she needs lots of sun to be happy. When whales fly, she'll be happy." Alex stood up and mussed Tut's hair as she walked past. "Thank you for saving my butt."

Ten

Tut was hungry again. He went into the house and looked through the kitchen. There was no milk, no bread, no fruit. He looked in the pantry and found a box of crackers and some peanut butter and three cans of peas. His grandmother had left them on her last *mercy* trip. That was what his father called them. Tut wished that you could rerun life like you can a movie, go back and change things, take words that were painful and wipe them away. When she went out the door that day, she'd turned and glared at her son. "I will not set one foot in this house again until I get an apology." She was so angry, she was shaking.

Tut's father had just smiled and said, "Hurrah!"

Tut didn't miss the cleaning ordeals and Gramma Esta wasn't a person that he could say he enjoyed, but she used to make sure that there were boxes of macaroni and cheese and cans of soup on the shelves. She made sure that he had clean clothes and his shirts were mended. She was like a stage manager, not one of the main actors in his life. Tut wished the two of them would make up. He was dead sick of crackers.

Tut started to pick up clothes that littered the floor. He gathered an armful and started the washing machine. As he worked, he dreamed about a steamed hot dog, with mustard and cheese sauce, onions and bacon bits. With a side order of crispy fries and an ice-cold root beer. Like the ones they used to get at the hot dog stand on the way to Portland.

He went back into the living room, grabbing some more crackers as he went through the kitchen, and thought about a really good seafood stew. Mr. White would give him a bowl of his chowder every once in a while. It was always thick with white flakes of fish, lobster, real cream, and butter melted on the top.

The first load of washing was done and he went out and hung the clothes on the line. The wind caught them and they snapped in the breeze. It wouldn't take them long to dry.

He looked up toward the hill house. He could hear voices, but he couldn't make out what they were saying. He went back inside, trying to remember every detail of the lobster bake he and his dad went to two summers ago. It was right down on the shore by the rocks. The clams and the corn were sweet and the lobsters bright red-orange and steaming hot. He'd ripped them apart and dipped the flesh in butter. He ate it sitting next to his dad and watching the waves break.

Back in the living room, he looked around and wondered what normal looked like. He pulled off torn slipcovers and threw them away, folded the old afghan and laid it across the back of the couch like his grandmother always did at her house.

There was a pounding suddenly at the back door.

"It isn't looking good up there," Alex said as she burst into the kitchen. "But today she's mad at Dave and not me. So that's a good thing." She went to the kitchen window and looked out to the bay. "Does anyone live on those islands, Tut?" she asked. She was talking about the three islands Tut called the Turtles. That's just what they looked like, green turtles in the sea.

He held up two fingers.

"Are some of them empty?"

Tut smiled. Islands weren't referred to as *empty,* but nobody would be living out there after the Labor Day weekend.

"Could someone live on those islands without anyone knowing it?"

Tut shrugged. There were camps on them. But they were only summer camps. They would be cold and drafty. The one that was out farther was too dangerous. It was beyond the current. Twice a day, when the tide changed, the river in the next town flooded out into the sea. The current was stronger than she could possibly imagine.

Tut could see her face reflected back in the pane of glass. She was only dreaming. He went back to thinking about food.

Oranges, big, juicy sweet oranges, he thought as he went to get another load of wash out of the machine. Alex helped him hang the clothing.

"Didn't anyone ever tell you about washing darks and whites separately?" she asked.

In his hand was a wet shirt. He surprised himself and threw it at her. The icy-cold shirt landed on her neck. She squealed, pulled it off, and threw it back. Soon wet clothes were sailing back and forth. Tut could throw them faster than Alex. Soon she was covered in damp laundry. She collapsed, laughing, to the ground.

"I give up, Tut," she gasped.

Tut nodded and then started thinking about Oreo cookies.

Alex went home to "take the pulse," as she called it.

Tut felt not only hungry but restless inside, hungry and restless. He walked quickly through the marsh and out to the point. The gulls were coming in behind the boats. They circled in a huge mass, looking as if they were connected by invisible strings. The fishermen waved to Tut as they passed. The last boat in was the *Merry Anna II.* His father's eyes were fixed straight ahead. He looked empty to Tut, sort of like the abandoned shell of a hermit crab.

As he watched, Tut wondered whose fault all this was. Why was he hungry when others were full? Why was his mother dead when Alex's mother, who seemed to think only of herself, was alive?

He went slowly to the harbor. There was a line of boats ahead of his father and he didn't have to rush.

Later, in the market, Tut waited with the catch.

"I caught me such a huge fish today," Mark O'Brien said dryly, "that I couldn't bring it on board. I was afraid it would swallow old Gunther here, so I had to cut bait or explain to Polly how I lost her father."

"When did all that happen?" Gunther asked cautiously.

"You know when you were peeing off the bow and I pulled back on the throttle? It was right about then."

Mr. Gunther snorted as the others laughed. There was a spirit there that Tut loved, the spirit of these men who spent most of their time fighting the sea for a living. They were alone most of the day and came together here, sharing their stories. There were fewer men fishing each year, and it seemed that there were fewer fish.

Tut's turn came and his father's fish were weighed. Mr. White reached into his drawer and handed Tut the money. Tut's father had once accused Mr. White of cheating, so they were always paid daily in cash. It had been a good catch and Tut took three bills, put them in his pocket, and walked over to where his father stood. By now he was so hungry that he felt weak.

He handed his father the rest of the money, then turned and walked away.

"Hey, Tut. Where you going?"

Tut just kept walking. His father called again and Tut turned. His hands moved in jerky short movements emphasizing every word he made, like he was screaming in sign language. He told him that he was hungry and he was going to buy food.

ELEVEN

TUT FLUNG OPEN the door to the old market. The floors were slanted, the aisles narrow and dimly lit. The smell of smoked meat and cheese hit him as he walked through to the deli. Mr. Baker stood behind the counter in his bloodstained apron. Tut wrote that he wanted two pounds of hot dogs. They came hitched together in long links. Mr. Baker folded them carefully and wrapped them in clean white paper. He looked over the top of his half glasses at Tut.

"Having a party?" he asked. His eyes were friendly.

Tut shook his head. He was mad and he wanted to stay mad.

"Anything else I can do fer ya?"

Tut just shrugged and walked to the vegetable counter, where he picked out onions, potatoes, and peppers. What else could Mr. Baker do for him? For a moment Tut thought about what it would be like if God ran a store, a branch in every town, where you could go in and order what you needed. He wondered if God looked like Mr. Baker. But Mr. Baker was always smiling and it didn't seem as if you could see the things God saw and still be that happy.

Tut picked out cheese sauce, bacon bits, big soft rolls, a half gallon of milk, and a bag of potato chips. He headed home, struggling with his load. His stomach was screaming now. Just north of the harbor he took out the hot dogs and ate two of them cold. The pain stopped. The shaky feeling faded.

The marsh was quiet. Over near the outlet he could hear the geese quibbling. They'd be flying away soon, looking like so many fine pen marks against the fall sky. Tut dreaded the winter.

When he reached home, his father was standing in the middle of the living room.

"You've been doing a lot of work around here, Tut," he said. "Looks nice."

Tut kept his back to his father and started cooking.

"You're mad at me," his father said. Tut put four hot dogs in a pan and looked at his father. He was sure that anybody with a lick of sense could see the mad in his eyes.

"Don't blame ya none. I haven't been much of a father lately. Haven't been much of a man, really." The words hung in the air unanswered.

Tut felt bad. Here he was madder than hell at his father because he'd been so hungry and it was the first time in weeks that his father seemed sober.

When the hot dogs were done, Tut smothered them with onions and peppers, cheese sauce and mustard, then went to find his dad. He was sitting on the back steps. Tut was about to open the screen door and hand him his plate when he saw him lift a bottle to his lips. Tut turned quietly and went back into the house.

He took two of the hot dogs and went upstairs to his room. Tut ate the first one quickly, then started on the second. He could hear his father start to sing in the backyard. Tut shut the door and pushed the heavy bureau over to block it. The slant of the ceiling would make it impossible for anyone to push it in from the outside. He'd seen the bottle. His dad always went a little nuts on vodka.

Tut sat by the window. The lighthouse beacon was pulsing against a drab gray sky out on Mosher Point. He heard his father enter the house. Soon he'd want Tut to play his Irish ballads while he sang along. It could go on for hours.

It started with his father calling his name. Then he could hear him climb the stairs and knock on the door. He tried the handle, and called Tut's name again. Tut had never shut him out like that before. He pounded harder and harder. Tut could hear the rage start to build. He buried his head under the pillow and pulled the covers over him. The noise went on and on.

He heard his father slump against the wall and slide down to the floor. Then Winston Tuttle started to sing in a beautiful tenor voice. It was an old Irish ballad about good-byes. The sun going down and the moon coming up and how the singer needed to find his way home. Tut listened. There was more to that song and Tut knew it well. The next sound he heard was a wailing, awful cry that always turned Tut's anger to pity.

The window was hard to open, but he got it up and crawled out on the shed roof. He walked the ridge pole to the end and climbed down the ladder. It was there for moments like this.

One thing Tut knew for sure was his father wouldn't move from that spot and he would sing and cry for a good part of the night. The clouds had broken apart into small fragments that ran over the face of the moon. Tut watched a trail of light that looked as if it came from the horizon right toward him.

"Your father has a beautiful voice." The words came from just feet away.

Tut jumped.

Alex and Willow came out of the shadows.

"You know what's weird about us, Tut?" she asked, not waiting for an answer, although he did have a list of things that he thought were weird about both of them. "The weirdest thing about us is that . . ." She looked across the bay and gasped. "Oh, Tut, look at that! Look at the way the light makes a trail straight across that island. It looks as if we could walk on it, doesn't it?"

It does look that way, Tut thought. *Of course if the current caught you, you'd be in Ireland listening to real Irishmen singing drinking songs.*

He watched Alex stare out to sea. She was unaware of his eyes on her face as the moonlight lit every surface.

"My aunt Joanie called today. She heard that Mom and I aren't getting along. She wants me to go live with her, but I really don't want to. She decorated a bedroom with teddy bears in pink tutus just for me. It's one of the worst nightmares I ever had. She lives in D.C." She finally fell silent and just watched the trail of light.

"Will you write about what's out there on those islands?" she asked.

Tut nodded.

Alex started to leave, then turned to Tut and whispered, "You know, don't you, that normal people are scared of the dark?"

Twelve

The first day of school was a warm Monday. Tut thought it would be easier to walk into that building and close the door if it was a dark, rainy day.

"Have you written about what's on the islands?" Alex asked him as they stepped onto the bus. He shook his head no. On Tuesday she asked again and on Wednesday, Thursday, and Friday. He didn't know what to write. Friday he promised that he'd have her note on Sunday. That gave him two extra days to worry about it. He couldn't just write what the islands were really like because they were covered with thick-growing evergreens and spotted with naked gray granite. Mosses grew on them, wild blueberry bushes, and deep beds of ferns. But in this note he had to make them sound desolate, hard, cold.

Saturday morning he went to work for Mr. White. He told him that he wanted to pay back the shoes. Mr.

White argued, but Tut just took the broom and started to sweep. That afternoon Alex went with him to Widow Banks. They cleared the garden for winter, pulling up the dead tomato vines and pepper plants. Then they raked the garden clean. When they were done, Widow Banks fed them. Alex asked the widow about the islands and Tut smiled when she said she knew little about them. He made Alex wait.

The sun was just a glow beyond the islands Sunday morning when Tut woke up. He ran wet fingers through his hair in the bathroom, then filled his pack with the supplies he'd need for the day. Tut packed enough lunch for two people and a dog.

He'd sat up part of the night writing three pages of tight, small script telling of all the dangers and hazards of the islands. How easy it would be to freeze to death.

He folded the note, grabbed his backpack, and walked up the hill. Tut had always hated the Shaws' house. It looked like a large glass-eyed bug as far as he was concerned. He could see his reflection in too many glass surfaces. His hair stuck up at odd angles. His pants were baggy. His jacket was two years old. Tut made a face at his reflection. He couldn't imagine living in a house with that much glass. It would be like living in an aquarium. There was no sign of Alex. But when he stepped on the deck, Willow came barking to the door.

Willow jumped up, her front paw hit the door's handle, the lever kind, and the door started to open. To Tut's horror, he was standing on the deck, with the door wide open. Alex's head popped up over the back of the couch in the living room. Her hair was wild. Her eyes puffy from too little sleep.

"Tut!" she squealed, and pulled a big blanket around her shoulders. "Excellent! Good morning. What time is it?" she asked, turning around to see the sun pouring up over the edge of the earth. Alex stretched in the cool morning air. The house was chilly and she pulled a sweater on over her pajamas.

"Sit," she ordered Tut, motioning toward the couch. Tut thought it sounded like an order that you'd give a dog. He didn't move.

"Please sit," she said.

Tut was wondering when Gwen and Dave would come running out of some room screaming about the early hour.

"They're gone," Alex said. "They said something a couple days ago about a folk festival in Brunswick. I guess that's where they went. Did you know that there are some parents whose children actually know where they are all the time?" Alex looked back at Tut, who hadn't moved. "Please, come and sit with me," she pleaded.

Tut pointed toward the door.

"You have to go?" she asked, looking suddenly lost.

Tut shook his head. He tried to sign what he wanted to say, but she didn't understand. She handed him a piece of paper and Tut wrote a note explaining that he wanted to go for a walk on Newcomb Beach.

"Can I come?" she asked as she ran off through the house, not waiting for an answer. "I'll be ready in a second."

Willow stood with her nose at the door. Tut opened it and they both went outside. Through the glass he could still hear Alex jabbering away as she got ready. Tut stood inhaling the cool air, watching the sunrise, and running his fingers through Willow's warm coat.

Finally Alex burst out of the door. "I'm ready," she exclaimed. Tut was glad to see that she had on sensible clothes. There were places where it might be downright cold. They started up through the marsh, then over the high stone ridge that changed suddenly to a wide expanse of rocky beach. The waves broke far out and Alex and Tut searched the tide pools for old buoys, strange pieces of driftwood, and shells.

Alex talked almost constantly. Tut didn't listen. He caught bits and pieces of her monologue. On the far side of the stone-covered beach, there was a large outcropping of boulders. You could just barely get around them at low tide; at high tide you had to go over the top. Alex climbed the rocks like a monkey, then just stood, looking toward the islands. Merrimen Island was the closest. Out farther was Greater Merrimen.

The breeze off the water made Tut shiver. He helped Willow up over the rocks. She seemed afraid of the dark holes between the stones and was distracted by the stench of rotten things buried in the seaweed.

On the farther side was a remote beach. It was too much trouble to get to. In all the years he'd walked there, Tut had only met one other person. He looked to see where Alex had wandered. She stood on the farthest edge of dry sand, dark against the gray-green water.

Willow ran to her, but Alex didn't pay any attention. Tut walked up behind her and finally threw a stone at the water. She turned to him as if waking.

"What?" she asked.

Tut motioned for her to follow him and walked to a wide piece of clear sand. *This is my beach,* he wrote in the sand. *On it no words can be spoken.*

"I don't know if I can do that," Alex said.

You must, he wrote.

Can I write? she wrote in the sand.

You can. But you can't write novels.

Okay. She smiled as she formed the letters.

It was a sandy beach and there were wet indentations around the rocks, formed by the tides. Tut looked up at the wide-open space and suddenly he had to run. Alex stayed with him, running just as fast as he did. He dashed around rocks and jumped over driftwood, and she was right there, or just behind him, or sometimes pushing ahead. Willow ran way out in front of them. When Tut had finally pulled ahead of Alex, he stopped. He picked up a flat, smooth stone and threw it through the waves. Once, twice, three, four times the rock skipped across the top of the water. Alex took one and threw it. Nine times it skipped across the surface before disappearing. Without saying a word, she did a dance that reminded Tut of an Indian war dance.

Willow chased the sandpipers and the gulls. When the sun was right above them, Tut looked for his perfect spot. Back by the side of the high dunes, there was a hollow in the sandy bank. He walked to it and dropped his backpack. He wrote the words *Fire* and *Eat* in the sand and then started dragging driftwood back to the spot. Alex helped him. They pulled big clumps of dried beach grass and Tut made tight rolls of it. He piled twigs on top, then lit the grass on fire. He added bigger sticks until he had a good fire burning.

Alex bit her lower lip. She wanted to talk so badly that it showed. When he smiled, she stuck out her tongue and then smiled back. They leaned against the dune and watched the waves breaking beyond the thin flames.

When the fire had burned down, Tut took two potatoes and wrapped them in foil and shoved them deep into the coals. Then he walked down the beach until he found a place where little bubbles had formed in the sand. He dug with his hands and motioned for Alex to do the same. She just looked puzzled until he pulled out a clam. Willow dug too, just because they were. When they had a pile of clams, they washed them in a tide pool. Tut wrapped them in a spare piece of foil and placed them on the coals. Next they roasted hot dogs on long sticks, holding them above the flames until they browned.

The hot dogs tasted good. The clams were sweet and tender; the potatoes were hot and mealy. Tut breathed deep, happy for the moment and the company. Then he looked through the flames and saw the islands out beyond the breakers. They looked so small to him, insignificant. He wondered if Alex was really serious about going out there. It would probably never happen. People said things all the time that never happened.

He pulled out the note. Hesitantly he handed it to Alex. She sat up straight reading his words. Her eyes danced with the descriptions of cold granite and thick spruce. He'd tried to make the camps sound more like barns than houses.

She wrote, *I could do it?*

You could, Tut wrote back. *But it will be lonely out there.* He brushed the sand clean and wrote, *There's no one to listen to your voice.*

Alex just looked at Tut. He could see her words without her writing them. Her life held so much evidence that it wouldn't really matter.

THIRTEEN

TUT WALKED with his hands deep in his pockets while Alex ran ahead of him down the beach. Did she understand what being on the island would be like? What about the fog? It could sit so heavy and thick that even though he knew where she was, he might not be able to find her.

She's such a child, he thought, watching her as she clambered up over the stone barrier. He could hear her start talking the minute she hit the highest stone. For just a moment he thought about turning around, but he couldn't. He walked toward the barrier reluctantly; on this side of it his silence didn't matter, on the other side it mattered a lot.

"I did it!" she exclaimed as he helped Willow up over the rocks. "I didn't think that I could be quiet that long, but I did it." She laughed. "That's the longest I have ever been quiet." Tut stood beside her. The waves were coming in high up the beach. The sea seemed wild suddenly, as if a storm was brewing offshore.

She turned to him and smiled, but Tut didn't.

"What's wrong?" she asked.

Tut sat down with his back to the wind and tried to write. *You aren't thinking about all the things that can go wrong. What about food and the cold? What about money to buy things you'll need? Where's that going to come from?*

She read over his shoulder as he wrote.

"I have some money," she said.

How much? he wrote.

"Some," she said.

What about the winter and the ice and fuel? he wrote.

"What are you talking about?" Alex exclaimed. "I'm not gonna spend the winter out there. I'm not an idiot."

Tut was utterly confused. *You said that you wished you could go out there and live until you were old enough to live by yourself,* he wrote.

"Well, I do, but I can't. I know that. What if my father comes to get me? Gwen was talking to him the other night." Alex sat down next to Tut, their faces just inches apart. "I heard her say that she'd raised me for fifteen years and now it was his turn. But it didn't sound like he wants me either." Alex closed her eyes tight. Her chin trembled. "I just thought that if he comes to get me, I could stay out there until he goes away. That's all, Tut. Just till he goes away."

They walked in silence back to Alex's house. Tut was thinking about all the things she'd have to take with her. Lanterns needed oil and heaters took fuel and Alex would have to have food. How long would a father who didn't want a kid in the first place wait around for her to be found? It could be a week. It might be two. It probably wouldn't be more than that.

At the edge of her driveway Alex stopped and looked at Tut. "I might not have to go. But if I do, I need to know you'll help me. Please say yes."

I'll think about it, Tut wrote.

"It will be like an adventure," she said, then ran toward her house, leaving him standing alone in the driveway.

An adventure in hell. Tut was sure of it as he started down the hill. Things like this always got screwed up. The Alex that he'd met that first day out on Sutter's Point wasn't who Alex was at all.

On the kitchen table was a note from his father. *Warning! Gramma Esta wants to negotiate a truce! She is on her way. Have gone to buy aspirin. Dad.*

Tut couldn't imagine how loud the first meeting between his father and grandmother would be. Besides, they were the ones who needed to talk, and Tut didn't want to have to listen. He stuffed the note in his pocket and bolted out the door.

Tut walked in deep shadow at the edge of the marsh. Willow had followed him as if it was the most natural thing for her to do. She looked more like Lady than ever. When he stopped, Willow leaned against his leg. Her warmth was as painful as it was comforting. *If I hadn't called for Lady, Mom would be alive,* he thought for the millionth time. Silence was not too huge a price to pay when he deserved so much more.

Tut forced his mind back to the practical problems of the day. What would Alex need on Merrimen Island? There might be some things in the cottage. Often people left stuff behind, canisters of sugar or boxes of noodles. Breaking and entering, that's what they'd be doing. He wondered what the fines would be.

When he got to the fish market, the doors were closed, but the light was on. Mr. White's pickup was parked in its usual place. Tut walked around the building to the back door and went in. He could hear the sound of a knife scraping shell. Mr. White looked up as Tut approached. In one of his hands was an oyster. In the other was a knife.

"The old girl wants oyster stew tonight," he said. "Sent me down here to get some fresh ones. Did I ever teach you the right way to shuck an oyster?"

Tut just shook his head. He had shucked countless oysters, but he let the old man teach him his way.

Mr. White handed him a short-bladed knife. "You hold it like this here," he explained, handing Tut a wide, icy-cold oyster. "Then you take the knife and force it in. Hold it so if the point goes wild, you don't make yourself a new belly button. Don't need two, you know.

"When you get the knife in there, you run it along the shell close to the surface as you can. You'll feel it when the muscle holding the shells together gets cut. Then you can pull 'em apart, like that!" Tut had done the same thing and there in his own hand was the flesh-colored body of the oyster.

"Oh, hell, you know how to do it already. Why do you let me go on like that, Tut?" Mr. White asked. "You like 'em raw?"

Tut nodded. He and his father had raw oysters whenever they could.

"Want to see who can eat the most?" Mr. White asked.

Tut agreed to the contest. So they sat there and fished the shells out of the big bucket, cutting them open and eating them until Tut's hands were numb from the cold and he couldn't stuff another one down.

Mr. White wiped his mouth with the back of his hand. "Well, now, I counted that you ate twenty-four to my twenty. I declare you to be the winner of this here contest, Tut." He leaned back in his chair. "You know what gives me a world of satisfaction?" he asked. "It's knowing that in some fine restaurant in New York City, what we just ate would cost some poor fella a day's pay. And just think, for us, it was practically free. Makes me feel rich. It does."

Willow slept at Tut's feet and for right now Tut felt peace.

Mr. White started shucking oysters again. "Why do people like oysters so much? They look awful. Don't they?"

Tut took the pencil that sat on Mr. White's desk and wrote, *Oysters taste like the sea.* That was why Tut liked them.

"Tut, I swear you got a poet living in that soul of yours." Mr. White looked closer at Tut, as if he was trying to read his thoughts. "You got something eating you." He wiped his hands on his apron, then pushed the paper back at Tut. "Out with it. Tell me now or I'll blab it all over South Marsh that you got a crush on Willard's wife. Ruin a man fer life if that kind of information got out."

Tut smiled. Willard Whitcomb's wife was one of the meanest and homeliest people Tut knew. Willard was in his eighties but kept fishing just so he could get away from her. Tut looked at the pencil for a moment and wrote, *I need to earn some money.*

Mr. White read what he'd written. "You having trouble?"

Tut just shrugged.

Mr. White eyed him. "Do you need money now?"

Tut shook his head no.

"You just want to work?"

Tut nodded.

"Tell you what. How 'bout you come in a couple afternoons a week? Then on Sunday you can wash the place down. Give it a good scrubbing like you did the other day. We'll have to keep it under the table. You're not supposed to be working till you're sixteen. Yer birthday ain't that far away. I was planning on asking you then if you wanted a job, anyway. It'll be good to have you around more."

Tut left the market and walked slowly through the

marsh. He didn't want to get home before things were settled. He knew once the fighting was over, his father would brew coffee and his grandmother would bring out one of her homemade pastries. He wouldn't mind coming home to that. As he came to his street he could hear voices that were loud and angry. But the noise was from Alex's house, not his.

Tut wondered what it must be like to be Alex. He knew he could make money and he'd save as much as he could to help her, but he took small comfort from that. In his heart, he wanted to do something right that minute to make the fighting stop.

FOURTEEN

MIDDLE OF SEPTEMBER.

IT ALWAYS SEEMED to Tut that Monday morning came crashing in on him like a cold, unwanted wave.

Alex was pounding at his door as soon as the sun came up. She walked around to the back and yelled to his window. When he finally came down, she was all ready to go. He stood at the door in his pajama bottoms.

"Hurry up! You're the one who wanted to walk instead of take the bus. We'll be late, for crying out loud!" she ordered.

Tut got ready, but he didn't hurry.

His grandmother left a huge bag of clothes for him. She knew every thrift store in a hundred-mile radius. In the whole bag there were about three things that he would wear. He picked a denim shirt and pulled it on.

School had been in session for nearly three weeks and

Tut had missed as many days as he could. The English teacher, Miss Berry, still worried him. Tut had spent the entire summer trying to avoid her. She'd caught him only once, in the widow's yard. He knew that she'd asked Widow Banks about him when he wasn't there. He could only imagine what the widow had told her.

"Will you hurry up, Tut? We have to leave now," Alex yelled up the stairs. "Dirt couldn't possibly move slower than you if it tried," she complained when he was finally ready.

The morning was cool as they climbed the first high bank of land toward the mainland. Tut hated the bus ride. He liked the sounds of the birds and wind so much better than the noise of people. The school was a mile and a half from Tut's house. He wished it was a hundred.

Alex was strangely silent as they approached the big sprawling building. Norman was standing outside the building with some of his friends when Tut and Alex crossed the parking lot.

"Hey, Tut. What you got, a girlfriend?" Norman sneered.

"Oh. Oh my God, Tut. Can it be?" Alex yelled. "The last time I saw anything that ugly, it was the orangutan's butt at the Washington Zoo. No, no, tell me it's not true," she yelled. "They've brought it here for show-and-tell. The ugly orangutan's butt from hell."

Alex was so theatrical, so animated, so funny. Norman turned beet red and the other students howled with laughter. Tut made a mental note: he never wanted to get the business end of Alexis Carlson.

For years Tut had spent a lot of energy trying to avoid Norman. This would make it impossible. Then Tut looked at Alex. She was just glaring at Norman as if he were dirt and she didn't give an owl's hoot if he was furious or not.

"What?" she asked, trying to read Tut's face. "Enjoy the moment, Tut."

He made it through math and history. He'd eaten lunch by himself. How many more days of this? he wondered. Maybe if he knew the actual number, it would be worse. English was the last class of the day. He sat at his desk, watching Miss Berry. Tut imagined music playing that sounded like it does in the movies, just before the hero is ambushed and killed.

"Last week I gave an assignment," Miss Berry said. Tut thought that she looked like an attorney pacing the front of the room. "I asked you to write about a special interest you have, and it seems that a few of you aren't interested in anything. So if you won't write, I will have each one of you stand up and tell the class your name and something about yourself. It can be a hobby or a passion that you have. Something." Groans came from all over the room.

Tut sat in the back. Two students ahead of him, Jessica Prentice was giving a glowing account of helping her uncle, a marine biologist, study bivalves. She sat down and then the student just ahead of Tut stood up. It would be Tut's turn next. The boy in front of him was done too quickly, and Tut hadn't heard a word he'd said. There was an uncomfortable silence. Then at the front of the next row Norman stood up and started to talk.

"It's not your turn," Miss Berry said. She turned back to Tut.

"He don't talk. He's stupid," Norman said.

Miss Berry glared at Norman. Tut could feel his own face burn. What did she want him to do? Sign words in the air?

"I don't want anyone to say anything like that in this class again." She drew out the words, giving them power as she spoke them. "Do I make myself clear?"

"But that's what my pa said. He says he's dumb," Norman declared.

"Norman, go to the office. Now."

Twice in one day Tut had been the reason for Norman facing humiliation. He wondered what torture Norman would come up with for him. With Norman out of the room, Miss Berry turned her attention back to Tut. He looked up into her face as she moved her hands.

"You know sign language?" she said as her hands formed the words.

Oh no, Tut thought. He could feel his cheeks burn. He looked around at the roomful of faces. Some of them he'd known all his life and some were bused in from other towns. Then there was Alex, sitting across the room by the window. She mouthed the word *communicate.*

I'm trapped. Just like a rat in a cage, he thought. The only other person besides his dad who actually knew sign language was a counselor who came once a month from Bangor. Tut always wrote down what he needed to say to teachers. He was never asked to participate this way. But if Miss Berry knew it, he'd have to answer her.

He started to spell out *T-u-t.*

"That's a nickname. I want your full name."

J-a-m-i-e T-u-t-t-l-e, he spelled slowly. To Tut it was like talking French when no one else knew the language.

"Good," Miss Berry said, and smiled. Tut was ready

to sit down. "Now tell us what it is you like to do most in the world, Jamie."

Jamie. His name sounded strange. Tut bit his lip. Jamie Tuttle sounded like a whole different person.

"Please tell me." Miss Berry expected something. He stared at her, wondering what it was she wanted.

"What do you like to do most in the world, Jamie?"

Read, he signed, and started to sit down.

"What kind of books?" she asked. "Who are the authors of the books that you like?"

He thought of the books he'd read. His mother's books. He signed a list of books by Jane Austen, C. S. Lewis, J. R. R. Tolkien, Edna St. Vincent Millay, Oscar Wilde, William Shakespeare.

"Did you understand those books?" she asked.

Tut thought for a moment. *I understood the words. But I don't always understand why people do what they do,* he signed, hoping with all his heart that was the end of her questions.

Miss Berry looked surprised. "Thank you," she said slowly. "I'd like to have you stay after class for just a moment. I won't take much of your time."

A bell sounded through the school and the other students left the room. Alex tried to catch his eye as she walked out, but he pretended not to notice.

"Come here, Jamie," Miss Berry said. "Have you read the poem 'Renascence,' by Edna St. Vincent Millay?" she asked as he walked to the front of the room.

Tut stared at the floor and nodded.

"If you could take that poem and boil it down to its purest essence, what is it about?"

He could hear Alex's voice in his head. She'd told him that teachers will leave you alone if you communicate with them. They think they're miracle workers.

He looked up into Miss Berry's face and wondered if he could trust her. *Spiritual rebirth,* he signed, not quite sure about how to sign the word *spiritual.*

"Bingo!" she said. "I'm going to be very honest with you, Jamie. I'm confused. According to these records it looks like you should have been kept back last year. Your scores are barely above third-grade reading level, yet what you've been reading is far beyond that. What you comprehend is higher still. Some of your writing is profound. In short, I don't know what to do with you."

Have you thought about ignoring me? he signed hopefully.

Miss Berry laughed out loud. "There's not a chance of that. I'm going to make an appointment for the counselor to run some tests. There are people in this village who are very fond of you. Mrs. Banks said that you've written some of the most beautiful poetry she's ever read. I'd like to see some of what you've written."

Tut stood and walked to the door.

"Jamie, I know that you aren't stupid. In fact, I think you are very bright. I will expect you to participate fully in this class." These were the last words he heard as he shut the door behind him. The halls were almost empty. Alex was waiting on the path.

"What did she want?" Alex asked.

He took the paper that she handed him. *She says that I'm not stupid,* he wrote.

"I could have told you that." Alex laughed and punched his arm.

FIFTEEN

END OF SEPTEMBER.

THINGS SEEMED to be different now in English class. On Wednesday, Miss Berry treated Tut as if he was the only student she had. When he finally left school, it felt as if electricity had been coursing through his body all day. Thursday morning he locked the door early and stayed in bed until Alex stopped pounding on the door.

He'd had enough communicating for the next twelve lifetimes as far as he was concerned. He spent the hours reading in his mother's parlor, curled up against a wall where he couldn't be seen through any of the windows. That afternoon, Alex found Tut sitting on the back steps, staring out across the bay, a book open in his lap.

"Boy, are you in trouble!" she said as she walked closer. "Miss Berry had this hotshot counselor drive all the way from Bangor to work with you today. She was really upset that you weren't there." Tut closed his eyes against the sound of her chatter.

"What's wrong?" Alex said, handing him the pad that she always carried.

Tut just shrugged.

"Tell me what's wrong. If we're going to be friends, we have to share our innermost thoughts."

He had spent so much time trying to bury his innermost thoughts that he wasn't quite sure what they were anymore.

You told me that if I communicated with them, they'd leave me alone. They haven't stopped talking at me since, he wrote.

"They'll get over it. They'll leave you alone eventually. Trust me. You just have to make them think you're okay. You're a mystery to them, Tut. Most people hate silence and you love it, so they think you're strange."

Do you think I'm strange? Tut wrote.

"Oh, I know you are," Alex said, looking intently into his eyes. "That's why I like you so much."

You're strange too, he wrote.

"Exactly." She grinned triumphantly. "What are you reading?"

Tut showed her the book. It was a worn copy of the Bible. The pages had been turned often. Many verses were underlined.

"Was this your mother's?"

Tut nodded. He remembered his mother sitting and reading it. She'd take a cup of tea into the parlor and curl up on the old couch and read. Tut would curl up at the other end and listen to her voice. If his father was late coming in, she'd read until she was sure he was safe.

"What part are you reading?"

Tut handed her the book and pointed to the verse that said *And the light shines in the darkness, and the darkness did not comprehend it.* That was what Tut felt God was like. He was light and answers. Tut believed there was a God. When the sun rose crimson in the sky, he could feel his soul inside himself move to meet the beauty of it. But he didn't know if he trusted God much. There were too many whys.

"What was your mother like?" Alex asked.

He motioned for her to follow him and led her through the house to the parlor. He picked up the picture of his mother and handed it to her. Alex studied the face.

"You look just like her," she said. It was Tut's face, but feminine and lovely; older, of course. She had two qualities that Tut knew he didn't have: she looked full of life and happy.

"You must miss her."

Tut stopped tears. He watched Alex as she gazed

around the room. It was just as his mother had left it. His father hadn't come into this room since the accident. Alex looked at the bookshelves and the pictures. There was one of Tut as a toddler in his mother's arms, one of Tut with a big fish. There was a picture of his mother and father together. She was in a wedding dress, a wreath of roses in her long hair, and he was in a black suit.

"Were they as happy as they look?"

Tut wondered. Had they been that happy? It was so hard to know. He wasn't sure if he remembered things as they really were or if death changed it all.

Tut walked out of the parlor and into the hallway. He had showed Alex all she was going to see today.

"Man, this place needs help," Alex commented.

Tut looked into the living room and wondered what she meant. Hadn't he cleaned the living room? The clothes he'd washed. The papers and magazines picked up. Alex moved down the hall and toward the kitchen. The floor was filthy, the sink full of dirty dishes. The counters were piled with boxes and papers and unidentifiable food.

"Looks like no one's done the dishes in years. Good grief!" she exclaimed, taking a closer study of the sink. "My God, is this tuna fish? It's purple! Oh, this is disgusting! Tut, you can die from having stuff like this around. Come with me," she ordered as she walked out of the kitchen and up the road to her house. She walked so fast that Tut had a hard time keeping up with her.

"Gwen, I'm home," Alex called.

"Don't bother me, for crying out loud. I'm in the middle of a mood," they heard Gwen call from her upstairs studio.

"When she's painting, all she seems to be able to do is scream. I think if something makes you that tense, you should probably find another career," Alex said. "Can you imagine what it would feel like to be important to someone?" Alex's eyes burned into Tut's.

He didn't know what to tell her. He couldn't imagine feeling this way now, but he could remember it.

"When we moved from Vermont, Gwen left all my stuff behind. Everything but my clothes, because she couldn't fit it in the car. She fit all of her things in the car. Come on, I'm starved."

Tut followed Alex into the kitchen. Alex reached up into the cupboard. The glasses were lined up perfectly. She pushed the blue ones aside and found two that didn't match.

"She thinks that if the house is in perfect order, everything is okay," Alex explained as she opened the refrigerator door. A bowl was filled with fish marinating in oil and spices. Eggs sat in a wicker basket that was shaped like a hen. Everything was clean and arranged like pieces of art, even the food in the refrigerator.

Alex grabbed a jar of milk and motioned for Tut to sit at the counter.

"Listen," Alex said softly. "I heard something today at school you should know. I went into the office and the door was open into the principal's room. The truant officer was there. He was talking about you and your dad. He said that your house is a mess and as far as he could tell, your dad was hardly ever home. And you've missed too many days."

Panic flooded Tut like a wave. He ran out the door and down the hill.

He looked around at the other houses. The lawns were mowed and the hedges trimmed. He needed to mow the rest of the lawn. He'd known that before, but he hadn't done it. Why hadn't he done it? Floors and dishes should be washed. He needed to make sure that their house looked normal.

He went in the back door and started to clean. He'd never really understood why people felt so compelled to sweep floors. If you just let the dirt pile up, after a while it didn't seem to get any worse. Alex stuck her head in the back door.

"You don't have to be afraid," she said. "There are plenty of things we can do." Alex rolled up her sleeves as she stood in front of the sink. She gingerly picked through the dishes and started to pile them on the counter. Plates in one pile, bowls in another, silverware in one of the bowls. Under the sink she found a dish drainer and soap. Soon she was washing dishes in soapy water.

"We can make it look like your dad's the best father in the world and no one will know," she said confidently. "If we get this place clean and you actually show up at school, they'll leave you alone. Trust me, Tut."

Tut wished he could be so sure.

The two worked in the kitchen until all the dishes were back in the cupboards. The floor was swept and washed. Tut's father would be home soon and Alex had to leave.

"I'll see you tomorrow," she said from the door. "It will be okay. You'll see."

Tut looked around. The counters were bare, but were they too bare? He thought about the bouquets of flowers at Alex's house. He opened up the door to the pantry and looked for something colorful to put on the table. His grandmother had brought a peace offering when she came. She didn't clean the house, but she'd stocked the pantry. The red and blue of a canned ham caught his eye. He took the can and, after polishing it with the dishcloth, placed it in the center of the kitchen table.

When he was finished, he walked to the harbor. The *Merry Anna II* wasn't there. He sat on Sutter's Point until dark. The wind off the ocean seemed warm compared to the air at his back. He walked down the streets of the village and checked the harbor again.

Tut knew where his father was. Two towns north there was a harbor twice the size of South Marsh. His father had a friend there that he often stopped to see on Thursdays. They'd have supper at the diner and eat corned beef sandwiches and drink dark ale. Tut had gone with him a few times. Thursday was the one night that Tut didn't worry if his father didn't come home. At least not as much.

SIXTEEN

FRIDAY AFTER SCHOOL Alex said she was going to go home and "play nice." She had been trying hard to get along with Gwen. Not every night, but too often, Tut could hear their voices. He wondered how long it would be until her father came for her.

Tut went off to work for Mr. White. He could feel the old man watching him. Finally Mr. White walked over.

"That new cop," he said. "The one who came here to get away from the city and can't talk about anything except how they used to do it in the city. You know the one?"

Tut nodded.

"If he fell off the end of the pier, with all them doodads he wears, he'd sink like a clam. Anyway, he was around here this morning asking a bunch of questions."

Tut glanced up at Mr. White's face.

"He asked how you were faring, Tut, and I didn't know what to tell him. So I lied like hell. I don't like to lie, but I'd hate to see what would happen if I told the truth. That is one tough spot to be in." He looked down at Tut, worry and sympathy mixed plain on his face. "Did I do right? Seems to me as if it's between you and your dad to work out. I can't see turning things over to a bunch of foreigners."

Tut nodded.

"I hope so. Doesn't seem as you could trust a man has to go around with that much hardware on, fer cryin' out loud," Mr. White muttered as he walked off toward the front of the market.

Tut was trying to figure out money. It had never been a big issue with him before. He'd lived without it and that was just the way it was. Now he'd have to save some of what he earned in case Alex needed something, but he also had to buy things for the house. Saturday morning he walked to Mr. Baker's store and bought soap, window cleaner, and paper towels. He bought a can of paint for the trim. Alex came down and watched him paint until she couldn't stand it any longer.

"Stop, Tut. For God's sake, stop!" she demanded. "Where did you learn to paint? You have more on you than on the wood. You're not supposed to paint the glass. Jeez!" She took the brush from him and started to work. "Go dust something," she ordered. "Why did you get this color?"

Tut shrugged.

"Was it on sale?" she asked, poking at the bright green with her brush.

He nodded and she got off the ladder and ran up the hill. She was back minutes later with a pail filled with white paint. She painted the house trim in quick, sure strokes. Tut borrowed her lawn mower and pushed it through the heavy weeds and grass. As he worked, he watched Alex paint.

At lunchtime Tut opened the canned ham, and Alex taught him how to make ham salad. There wasn't any mayonnaise in the fridge, so she used tartar sauce. They sat in Tut's kitchen and ate.

"Everything you eat starts with an *h*," Alex complained. "Hot dogs and ham. You need to branch out."

How about octopus and squid? Tut signed, knowing that not being able to understand him would drive her nuts.

"Write that," she ordered. When he refused, she said, "I'm going to ask Miss Berry to teach me sign language so you can't do that anymore." Tut gave her an outrageous grin.

Alex rinsed the plates off in the sink. "I heard Gwen

talking to my father again last night. She told him that Dave won't move in because he doesn't want a woman who's got an adolescent daughter with a mouth. She said I'm ruining her chance for happiness. I've been trying to be nicer. It seems like nothing I do can make it okay. Gwen's like that. When she's done with something, she's just done."

Where is your father? Tut wrote.

"His money always comes from the same address. Somewhere in the middle of the country—Chester, Missouri. His wife doesn't want him to be involved with us. So he just sends checks every month." She sighed heavily and looked at Tut. "The only thing I can think of that would be worse than wandering all over the country would be having to live in Missouri. Sounds like 'Misery,' doesn't it?"

She leaned against the sink and looked out the window. "He's never even asked Gwen for a picture of me. How can someone have a kid and not care what they look like?"

Tut could tell by the sound of her voice that she'd been wondering that for a long, long time.

"If he does come to get me, the night before he comes, we can take your father's boat and go out to the first island. Merrimen Island, isn't that what you said?"

Tut nodded.

"You can drop me off. Then every couple of days you can take the boat and bring me out things: oranges and apples and chocolate cookies." Tut could see the reflection of her face in the glass. From where he stood, her face was transposed right over the island that stood out so dark in the pale water.

Tut took the pad of paper and started to write. *What if he won't go away till they find you?*

"You don't have to worry about that. I think it will be the happiest day of his life if I just disappear." Alex scrubbed the counter.

Tut put things away in the fridge and thought. The summer people were gone; they were of no concern. *You'll need to be careful about the fishing boats.* She would have to hide from them. The fishermen were trained to observe everything. They watched the islands like a bunch of gossipy neighbors, but that constant awareness was what had kept so many of them alive.

Tut still didn't like the idea. Besides breaking into a camp, there was no guarantee that her father would pick a good day to come and get her. What if the ocean was rough that night? Alex loved the ocean, but she didn't *know* it. Knowing it and loving it were two different things. Tut knew that it could put you to sleep with its gentle rocking and the next minute pound the life out of you. You could love it, but you couldn't trust it. You had to read it like you would a book, paying attention to every single word.

We'll be okay if there's a full moon. If the harbor patrol is off for the night. If no one sees us. Tut sighed. Something had changed in the way he felt about Alex. He had gone from wishing she'd go away to listening for her at his back door. If he didn't see her, he missed her. If she was on the island, at least she'd be near. He wasn't happy about her plan to live on the island, but he hated the idea of her being dragged off to Missouri.

His father was still sleeping Sunday when he walked out the door into the early morning fog. It would burn off by ten. He had to get away and think.

Tut was only a few feet from the house when he heard Willow bark. Dave must be up for the weekend. Alex said she was going to bake brownies for him, see if she could win him over the traditional way.

Can't bear to miss a walk, can you? Tut thought, watching the dog. She ran ahead, turning every few yards to make sure that he was coming.

"Hey, Tut," Mr. White's voice called from the dock. "Got me an extra couple of doughnuts. If you don't eat 'em, I'm going to feed 'em to the gulls."

Tut smiled. The old man knew how to get to him, didn't he? Tut would do anything to deprive the gulls of food. He took the bag of doughnuts.

"Seems good to see you with that dog," Mr. White said.

Tut turned quickly and headed toward the point. He ate the doughnuts, breaking off pieces and handing them to Willow as they went.

He took one of his bottles and swung it around over his head. He'd written his mother about fixing up the house, trimming back the roses, and the way Alex looked as she'd painted the trim. He let the bottle go and it arched up high into the sky. He wondered if Alex would be okay on that stupid island.

"What do you write in those letters?" Alex's voice came from close behind.

He jumped, took a piece of paper from the pad she handed him, and wrote, *You walk just like a freaking cat.* He tore it into bits and threw it into the wind.

"Okay, don't tell me," Alex said. She pulled her coat tighter around her.

Tut handed her the last doughnut. He was standing beside her, mulling over every single thing that could go wrong, when she pushed him. He was off guard and he fell over into a big hummock of sea grass.

"Ha," Alex yelled, "gotcha!" She started to run back

along the path, screaming with delight as Tut chased her. Willow barked excitedly. Tut thought about what he'd do if he caught her. Tackle her? He stopped. She ran gracefully, leaping over rocks. Tut smiled. Watching her run was like watching the fluid gray arc of a wave just before it crashes onto the shore.

Seventeen

MONDAY, TUT'S NAME was called in homeroom and he was told to go to the office. The counselor was there with a case full of tests. It might as well be filled with ancient torture devices as far as Tut was concerned. If he had known she was going to be there, he would have stayed home.

The room they used smelled of disinfectant and mildew. Its walls were an awful green. A tiny window looked out on the parking lot. Tut sat so he could see out the window while the counselor talked about the tests that she was going to give him.

About an hour after they started, Miss Berry stuck her head in the door. "How is it going?" she asked.

The counselor handed her the latest tests that he'd taken. It had been a bunch of the easiest math questions Tut had ever seen. One question was, *If you have five balls and I take away two balls, how many balls do you have?* Tut had written, *I only have two balls.* Miss Berry looked seriously at the paper, then started to laugh.

"I don't know why you've been such a brilliant underachiever. But you have mastered the art." There was a sense of fun in Miss Berry's voice. She bent close to Tut and looked him straight in the eyes. "Listen, Jamie. I enrolled in a refresher course for sign language. I spent half my summer so I could understand you without you having to write out everything you wanted to say. I did that after meeting you last year and knowing you were going to be one of my students. Now I'm asking you to do this for me. I need to understand what you're capable of so I can know if I should be giving you fifth- or twelfth-grade work. It's obvious you hate testing. I can see that oozing out of every pore of your being. I don't blame you. But please, I need this as a guide. Will you promise me you'll try?"

Tut nodded reluctantly. In his economy, if she'd spent money on a class, then he owed her something.

Miss Berry looked through the counselor's material. She pointed to some tests for tenth and twelfth graders.

"But he's never succeeded above a sixth-grade level," the counselor said.

"Maybe that's because the other tests bored him to

death. His math teacher gave me this to show you. Look at the answers on this paper," Miss Berry said, handing her one of the previous week's assignments.

Tut could feel himself turn red.

"They're all wrong," said the counselor.

"Divide them all by two. If you do, you'll find they're all right. And there are no figures on the paper. He did it all in his head. He's read most of Shakespeare's plays, and he understood them. To sit and read them all, you'd have to understand them, wouldn't you? I want him tested without any of the limits that were imposed in the past. In fact, I want him tested as if he had no past record and you expected him to be brilliant."

Brilliant. The word bit into Tut's mind. It wasn't an adjective that had ever been applied to him before. It felt like a tight coat, uncomfortable and itchy.

"Okay," the counselor said, looking at Tut a little differently.

Tut made it through the rest of the morning's tests without any more problems. He did try to do his best and doubted very much if the word *brilliant* would ever be applied to him again. The afternoon was supposed to be spent doing personality testing.

Alex corralled him in the hallway after lunch. "The last school I went to, I was in the counselor's office all the time. They gave me every test on the planet. If they show you the ink spots, they'll try to figure out how well-adjusted you are by what you see in them. That kind of thing. Try and find nice things, Tut. If it looks to you just exactly like an evil cow, tell them it's a puppy. When they ask you how you feel about something, for God's sake, if you ever thought of killing anyone, don't tell them. And whatever you do, if they ask you to draw something, never use black crayons."

EIGHTEEN

IT DAWNED ON TUT that if he didn't show up at school, they now noticed. So he went every day and spent most of his time worrying when the results of the dumb tests would come. He didn't know why that bothered him so much, but it did. What would they find? By Friday there was still no mention of them, and Tut went to work at the market anxious and stewing about it.

Saturday afternoon Gwen was going to take some of her paintings to galleries in Portland. Alex asked to go along.

"I'm going to keep my mouth shut if it kills me," she told Tut. "I'll be so sweet, she'll think she has the wrong child with her."

Tut helped carry the paintings to the car.

"What do you think of them?" Alex asked when Gwen went back into the house for more. He wasn't an expert on art by any means, but he knew this much: Gwen had missed something in the translation of water and light to canvas. There were too many good artists in Maine and gallery space was prized. Tut knew before they left that Gwen would not come back in a good mood.

Tut decided to start pulling the weeds that filled the garden. With the lawn mowed, it looked like they'd fenced in the weeds on purpose. He was putting them in a pile in the far corner, starting a compost heap like the widow's.

He'd been working a short time when his father came out of the house. Tut just kept on pulling and carrying the weeds to the pile. Going back and getting more. His father pulled a handful of weeds and then another. Tut stole a look at him and realized that he hadn't really looked at his father in days. He had on a T-shirt without sleeves. His arms were browned by the months of summer sun. Tut looked at his own fair hands and wondered how he could possibly be Winston Tuttle's son.

"I got a call just now from your grandmother. She wants us to come down to dinner. You up for that, buddy?"

Tut looked into his father's eyes. There were so many things to reason through before he could answer.

"Don't you want to go? She says she turned out the best roast pork she's ever made."

Will you fight? Tut signed. He remembered his grandfather saying, "They're like cats. Neither one of 'em has brains enough to shut up."

"I will promise you," his father said, "that unless she says something I can't let go of without bursting a main artery, I'll ignore it. Maybe we can have a quiet meal with your grandmother. Let's finish this up and go eat."

They worked side by side, pulling the weeds and piling them high. His father started to hum. In the middle of a song he stopped and knelt on the ground. Tut walked over to stand beside him.

"Your mother looked all over the state for hollyhocks the same color as the ones her mother had when she was a girl. She planted those the year before she died. I never thought they'd come up in this mess."

Tut watched his father pull the weeds carefully away from the rounded leaves of the hollyhocks. He even pulled the tiny grass blades away. "They should be pretty next year."

Tut was still amazed at how things like that made him happy and sad. It was like he could never feel a pure emotion. They were always colored with a different feeling. It was good to see something she'd planted live on.

When they were done, they washed and dressed and then started down the coast to Gramma Esta's. They drove through small towns that were formed around harbors, past churches with white steeples pointing up into the clouded sky, around the golden marshes. Tut's father was quiet; his fingers held the steering wheel. His knuckles showed white where he held on so hard. Tut wanted to know what he was thinking.

Dinner was ready when they arrived. Gramma Esta always served wine with her meals, but today the glasses held water. Steam rose up from the mashed potatoes, and the scents of garlic and roast pork filled the whole house. They were almost finished when Esta started in.

"I hear the lawn is mowed. It's something when old friends call up to announce that the lawn is finally mowed. Like it's the Olympics or something."

"Tut's been doing a lot around the house lately," his father said. Tut watched as the color in his cheeks started to change. A muscle in his jaw twitched just slightly. This was how it always began.

"Well, somebody has to," Gramma Esta said. Tut wanted to nudge his grandmother under the table. "So, how have you been?"

"Good. Been busy, is all." Winston took a long sip of water.

"Too busy, if you ask me. You got no time to come

see your mother. From what Mabel says, you ignore the boy. You weren't raised that way, Winston."

Tut slurped his milk loudly. Esta hated that and he hoped she'd turn on him. She didn't notice.

"What do you think, fifteen-year-old boys raise themselves?" she went on. "What if your father and I just stopped taking care of you when you were that age? Besides, the boy hasn't been right since Anna died." At her words, Tut could feel a rush of anger himself.

He watched his father's face. *Ten, nine, eight,* he started the countdown.

"Just because your wife is dead doesn't mean your son stopped needing you. And if I have to cook twelve pork roasts for you to hear that, I'll cook them. I hate to hear of the boy waiting for you to crawl out of a bottle long enough to notice he's still breathing. Everyone in that village feels sorry for you. Poor Winston, I hear. Poor Winston. What about your son?"

Tut watched the muscles of his father's jaw twist beneath the skin. *Seven, six, five.* His father looked across the table into Tut's eyes. Tut wondered how many arteries in his father's body were popping. Tut nodded toward the door. His father nodded. Tut held up four fingers. *Four, three, two, ONE.* They stood up and bolted outside.

"Hey, get back here! You two get back here right this

minute," they heard her yell, but they ran through the yard and jumped into the old black Ford. The pickup lurched into gear and started forward. Tut's father looked at him. His eyes blazed with the pain. If only Gramma Esta knew when to shut up!

"I didn't fight with her, but it cost me, Tut. Sometimes I think Dad died out of self-defense. The doctor said it was like his heart just blew up." He ran his hand over his own chest. "I think I know how he must have felt just before that sucker let go."

Instead of heading north, the truck turned south and they went out one of the many fingers of land that jutted into the sea. The road meandered over narrow bridges and across the backs of islands. Seeing his father's profile against the light and sea made Tut feel safe. He didn't need to know where they were going. They stopped at a store and his father bought a soda for each of them, a candy bar for Tut, and bait. They drove till they came almost to the end of the land. Winston stopped the truck in a wide sandy pull-off.

In the back were casting rods. Tut carried the rods while his father carried the tackle box and bait down the trail to the beach. The wind was cool off the water. The sun was low in the west behind them. It made their shadows long on the sand.

They walked until they came to just the right spot. There was a bend to the beach and they fished from there. His father handed Tut an eel and he stuck a hook through its head. He pulled back on the rod and then swung it forward. The bait sailed through the air, and the line sang off the reel. It landed just about where Tut wanted it to.

"Nice cast, Tut." His father cast out too. His tall boots and jacket smelled like fishing and fresh air. He sat down on the sand next to Tut.

"The reason I didn't fight with your grandmother back there was that she was right. I know that." He stared hard at the waves for a long time, then looked at Tut straight on. "I've been using Anna's being dead for an excuse long enough."

Tut marveled at the power of the word *dead.* Seven years ago, the day after the accident, his father had taken him for a walk out to Sutter's Point. His face was different that day. He looked out into the waves and said, "Your mother is dead." Tut remembered that it started out sharp and painful, but it hadn't stopped there. It had grown until the shadow of it colored Tut's whole world.

They fished until the moon rose and the tide pushed them up the sand. They stopped at Gramma Esta's on the way back home and Tut ran into the house and left a big striper as a peace offering. It was very late when Tut finally crawled into bed, tired and practically drunk from the salt air and being with his dad. And then he thought of Alex.

NINETEEN

BEGINNING OF OCTOBER.

TUT'S WORLD felt twisted in so many different ways. He knew that some things were good. His father had started getting himself up in the morning. As far as he could tell, he hadn't had anything stronger than coffee since the day before the dinner at his grandmother's. That was a very good thing, but Tut had no confidence it would last.

Alex was expecting him to help her and he knew that he would. She gave him daily accounts of her mother's mood swings. The trip to Portland had been a disaster. One gallery owner had laughed out loud at her mother's pictures. Another had asked if they were paint by number. She'd taken it out on Alex all the way home.

Miss Berry was expecting Tut to give her something more in class every day. He felt like he was under a microscope.

"I want you to stay after class today, Jamie. Will that be a problem?" Miss Berry asked toward the end of class.

It had to be about the tests. Tut sat in his seat after the last student left. Miss Berry smiled at him. He didn't smile back.

"Do you know what average is on an IQ test?" she asked.

Tut nodded. He knew that average was a hundred.

"I want you to guess what your score was."

One hundred, he signed, and then glared at her, trying to read her face. Tut hated guessing games.

"Guess again," she said, her eyebrows raised. She was enjoying this.

Up or down? he signed.

"Up," she said casually.

One hundred and five. He moved his hands to make the signs.

She shook her head no.

One hundred and ten.

"Nope."

One hundred and fifteen.

She folded her arms across her chest and shook her head.

One hundred and twenty. Tut could accept average or just a little above. He was afraid of being more.

"One forty-five, Jamie!"

I cheated, he signed.

"You know you didn't cheat. You're obviously very intelligent, Jamie," she said, smiling. "You're not comfortable with this at all, are you?"

Tut was feeling wounded somehow. How could this be? He couldn't spell all that well. Stupid Tut. He'd always been called *stupid* Tut. Miss Berry was going on about new ways of thinking, independent study, books, reports. He just wanted to run out the door.

"The tester also found some LDs, learning disabilities, that have masked your potential." She looked at him and Tut realized that the panic inside him was showing. "Jamie, this is nothing to be afraid of. This is a good thing."

Miss Berry was smiling like an idiot now. "I want to stop by your house this evening and talk to your father. He needs to know about this as soon as possible. It will make it easier on you if he understands what's happening."

Tut felt sick. He nodded and headed for the door.

"Jamie." Miss Berry put her hand on Tut's shoulder. "What this means is that you have the capacity to do amazing things. You can waste it if you want. It's entirely up to you."

Tut walked out of the building. The trees had changed

early this year and most of the leaves were on the ground. He could remember his mother taking him for a walk on this very road; a thick carpet of fallen leaves had covered the tar. Sunlight had poured down on them and they'd walked side by side, kicking the leaves with every step.

"This is the scent of fall, Jamie," she'd said. He smelled it now. It was the same smell of rotten leaves, sweet fern, and salt air. He wished he could talk to her now.

There was a stone wall beside the road. He climbed over it and lay down out of sight of the world. Tears came and the deep breathing turned to sobs. He heard a car drive away and between the stones saw that it was Miss Berry. She had no idea what she was doing to his life.

Tut wiped his face on his sleeve. Miss Berry was going to his house to talk to his father. Could there be anything worse? He vaulted the wall and broke into a steady run. Alex and Willow were waiting for him on the back steps.

"What happened?" Alex asked.

Tut wanted to hit something.

"Why are you so upset?" Alex's brows were creased with worry.

Miss Berry's coming here to talk to my father TONIGHT, he wrote.

"Oh my God! Why?" she asked.

She wants to talk to him about the test scores. He's never gone more than five days without drinking. That's his record. What if she comes and he's . . . Tut couldn't finish writing the sentence.

"Okay, okay," Alex said. "We have to set the stage. We can get supper cooking, stuff like that. Maybe your dad will be sober, or maybe he passed out on the boat," Alex added as if that was a positive alternative.

Tut wrote, *Or looking on the bright side, maybe he drowned.*

Alex read the words. "I'm sorry. I'm just trying to help."

Tut didn't have any idea when Miss Berry would be there. He swept the kitchen floor. Alex vacuumed the living room. Tut walked through and checked everything. The bathroom was clean. It looked okay to him anyway. Alex pushed past him and refolded all the towels.

She looked around. "Let's get supper cooking."

Tut went to the pantry and took a can of cream of mushroom soup and one of tomato and mixed them together in a saucepan.

"You don't have any idea how gross that is, do you?" she asked.

Tut just poured in two cans of milk and kept stirring the soup, trying to get rid of the creamy white lumps.

At dusk a car turned into the driveway. Alex let Miss Berry in. Tut prayed that she'd turn around and go home when she saw that his father wasn't there. Didn't teachers have lives of their own?

"Hi, Alex. How are you? Who is this?" she asked, pointing at Willow.

"That's Willow," Alex told her.

Miss Berry sank to her knees and patted the dog.

Alex stood behind her, trying to signal to Tut. She could see his father coming up the street. The look on her face showed plainly what shape he was in.

Tut watched as Miss Berry looked around the house. Her eyes went to the parlor and she stood up and walked into the room and started looking at the bookcases.

"Were these your mother's books?" she asked.

Tut nodded. He leaned against the wall in the hallway and waited. He heard footsteps in the shed. The kitchen door slammed open and there stood his father with the biggest codfish Tut had ever seen resting on his back. Tears were streaming down his father's face.

"This is it, Tut!" he wailed, leaning down and flinging the fish onto the table with a huge thud. "It's the last damned codfish." He collapsed into a kitchen chair. "I knew," he continued between sobs, "that someday some bastard was going to catch it. I didn't want it to be me, Tut. I swear I didn't want it to be me. But the bugger was dead when I pulled him in. There was nothing I could do!" Finally he looked up and noticed Tut with his head buried in his hands and Miss Berry standing there with her mouth open.

"Who . . . who are you?" he asked.

"Jamie's teacher."

"Shit!" he said, as if conferring face-to-face with the fish. "Would you care fer a cup of cod?" he asked her.

"I'd love a cup of tea," she answered, taking off her coat as if she planned to stay.

Tut's heart sank into his shoes. She did stay. She made tea, good strong tea, and gave some to Tut's father. She helped Alex warm up the unusual soup. Tut set the table. While Winston Tuttle told them the whole story of the decline of the great codfish, Alex and Miss Berry acted as if this, being the last one, was a thing to mourn. It lay across the middle of the table, staring blankly with one eye at the ceiling. As they all sat around the huge fish, eating soup and crackers, it reminded Tut of a strange wake. He couldn't swallow. While the others talked and ate, Tut just wished that he could trade places with that cold dead fish.

Finally, after they'd eaten and the fish was removed to the shed, Tut's father made his way to the couch and quietly passed out. Miss Berry didn't say very much. Tut wanted her to tell him exactly what she was thinking and what she planned to do about it.

"Will you be okay tonight?" she asked.

Tut nodded. He'd be fine.

She put on her coat and was headed out the door when she turned to Tut again. "Are you sure?" she asked. "I hate leaving you like this."

We'll be fine, he signed.

The next morning Miss Berry was back there early. Tut heard her voice downstairs before he was out of bed. He tried not to listen, didn't want to listen, but heard anyway.

"Mr. Tuttle, you have a problem and you need help, for Jamie's sake if not your own."

"Tut's doin' fine."

"Jamie is doing fourth-grade work when tests show he should be at the top of his class. Jamie is silent when from all of the doctor's reports, there is no reason why he shouldn't be able to speak. He is depressed and worried and acts more like a forty-year-old man than a fifteen-year-old boy."

"This is really none of your business," Tut heard his father say.

"I'm Jamie's teacher and I'm making it my business, Mr. Tuttle."

Their voices quieted down and Tut couldn't hear any more that was said. Finally, after a half hour, he heard doors slam and a car engine start and Miss Berry drove away.

TWENTY

WHEN TUT WENT downstairs, his father was sitting at the kitchen table. He had a piece of paper that Tut recognized as a poem he'd turned in days before. Miss Berry had asked the class to bring in their favorite poems and Tut had brought in his second favorite. He wasn't sure that he'd share his favorite poem with anyone. His father read the poem as Tut searched for coffee that he knew wasn't there. He finally sat down across from his father and watched as he read the poem one more time. When he rubbed his chin, it sounded like sandpaper.

"Well, that Millay woman knew how to write poetry, didn't she?" He sighed heavily as if he was pulling air up from his toes. "Was this from one of your mother's books?" he asked Tut.

Tut nodded.

"Your teacher just chewed me out with words from a book that belonged to your mother. Huh! It's almost like having Anna come back and bawl me out herself. Would be just like her. We were in the middle of a fight the day she died." Tut's father stopped and bit his lip just a minute before he went on. "I was mad at her because she'd bought a load of groceries for the Bridges. She was always doing so much fer people, and sometimes we couldn't afford it. I was getting the new boat and it scared me, paying so much for that. I took it out on her." He looked at Tut with painful eyes. "The last words I said to her were mean, Tut, and I have regretted them every day since."

Tut waited. There were two ways that this could go. Two ways that were very different and Tut held his breath.

"This poem, 'To the Wife of a Sick Friend,' is this how your life feels to you?" his father asked.

Tut sat still as the words of the poem rolled through his mind, declaring how bad life really hurt. He tried to think what to say. If he said yes, what would his father's reaction be? If he said no, it would be a lie. He thought about the codfish, stiff and cold. He was jealous.

His father stood up so quickly that his chair flew back, crashing on the floor. "Damn it, Tut!" he yelled. "I'm asking you to tell me the truth. Is that how your life feels? I want to know, because that's how my life feels and I'm so sick of being alone and feeling this way."

Tut raised his hand and cupped his fingers, then bent his wrist down twice. Yes, yes, that *was* what his life felt like for as long as he could remember.

Mom wouldn't want that, Tut signed. *She wouldn't want us to hurt this bad. She'd forgive us.*

"It's forgiving myself that I find so hard. Can you get me the book that poem came from? I'd like to read more."

Tut walked into the parlor and took the thin volume from the shelf. He felt funny sharing it with anyone. There was a great reluctance to hand over the book. He wondered at that feeling even as he placed it in his father's hand.

Tut opened the refrigerator and stood staring at the contents. Nothing seemed to go together for a decent breakfast. He kept glancing at his father as he thumbed through pages.

"Come on," Winston said a little later as he looked around the kitchen. "Let's go down to the diner an' see if Betsy still makes the worst coffee in New England."

Frost sparkled in the light from the headlights. The heater hadn't had time to warm the cab of the pickup. Tut shivered as they pulled into the parking lot.

"Hey, what in blazes brought you out?" Betsy was a square-built woman. Her gray-brown hair was braided and then wound around her head. "We haven't seen your face in the light of day fer half a century."

"We just came to see if the coffee is as bad as it used to be," Tut's father said, and some of the regulars laughed.

"Damn good to see ya out, Win," Betsy said, leaning close and whispering to his dad. His father ordered them both eggs and ham. Tut had two eggs over easy with dense slices of fresh-made bread that he smothered with strawberry jam.

His father said he was going out in the boat but to read and not to fish. Tut wondered what the words of the other poems would do to him. Edna St. Vincent Millay wrote words that pointed to the inner things. It was like she held up a mirror and showed you your own outrage. What would Tut's father do with that?

After they were done eating, Tut's father drove him to school. What would Alex think, arriving at his house only to find him gone? He was late, but he didn't care. When he got to math class and sat down, he glanced across the room. Alex looked as if she was in a world of her own misery.

What's up? Tut wrote when they had a chance to be alone.

"Gwen and Dave had a fight last night. She wants him to move up here permanently instead of just visiting here and there, but he wants to stay in Portland. I don't know what the big deal is. Anyway, after she was done screaming at him, she called my father."

What did she say?

"I don't know. All I heard was his name and then she closed the door."

Three days later they took the long way home after school, across the wide-open fields, through the house-lined streets, then followed the twisting, narrow road that led down to the harbor. Behind them a siren started to wail. It grew louder, stronger. They climbed up the bank beside the narrow road and watched as an ambulance came into sight and sped by, lights flashing.

"I hate those things," Alex hissed as it sped out of sight.

As they turned the bend in the road, they could see where the flashing lights had stopped. It was at the harbor. They ran to see what had happened. What if it was Tut's father? There were so many times that he'd worried about this very thing. He'd imagined the boat being towed in and his father hurt or worse. He prayed it wasn't him, then felt guilty that it might be someone else's dad. Tut and Alex pushed their way through the crowd of men in canvas jackets, heavy denim jeans, and black rubber boots. The uniform of the fishermen.

Tut found Mr. White in the crowd. They stood side by side and watched the medics as they worked. It was Tyler Burke. He had a daughter, Ashley, in the class just behind Tut and a brand-new baby boy. Tyler had been bragging about him just days ago. Now his lips were shut in a tight grimace, his face was gray. Tut could read the pain in his eyes. The medics were cutting away his coat. He turned paler still and passed out.

"Got caught in his own damned net," Mr. White muttered. "Was out there fishing alone. He was stuck there till somebody could cut him loose. That'll be the end of his fishing. He'll lose that arm on account of this. You can't even bait a snot-bloomin' hook with one arm!" Mr. White spat on the damp gray planks of the pier and headed back to his shop.

Tut didn't want to have the images of Tyler Burke's suffering in his mind. He turned away from the crying wife, the sober faces of the other fishermen, and the weird quietness of the crowd.

His father's boat was in the harbor. Tut searched the crowd and couldn't see him anywhere. It could mean his father was at the house or a bunch of other things Tut didn't even want to think about. Without any explanation to Alex, Tut started to run for home.

The door was slightly open into the kitchen. There was bread on the counter. He looked in the pantry. The shelves were stocked with crackers and flour, sugar and tea. There were cans of fruit and vegetables. Tut opened the refrigerator. There was milk, butter, eggs, and bacon.

Tut heard a noise in the front of the house and walked into the hall. His father was in the parlor. He looked up when he heard Tut.

"I haven't been in here for years. She was so strong in this room, it seemed as if I couldn't bear to be in here."

He'd shaved. His eyes were looking better, not quite so wounded and sad, not hungover, just clear and blue against the dark lashes.

"I made an appointment to see your teacher. I need to apologize for a certain codfish episode."

Tut just leaned against the doorway, feeling paralyzed by his father's presence in that room. Tut had made such an effort to put everything back just as it was. Just as she had placed it. He noticed that the picture of his mother, the one of her and Lady in the boat, was gone. Everything else seemed the same, yet was so horribly different. He walked out into the kitchen to draw his father away.

"I'm going now," his dad said. He was standing at

the door, waiting. "Tut, I have lost track of the times that I promised you I'd change. I can't say I won't slip up now and then, but I'm trying. I bet you that teacher of yours will go up one side of me and down the other. Do you want to come?"

He had no desire to go anywhere; he wanted to stand in one quiet place and think. The truck started and Tut listened to the fading sound of the engine. He stared at the counters: his father had washed the few dishes that had been left there, the floor had been freshly swept. Tut felt so strange. Why didn't any of this make him happy?

Later that night Tut heard Alex at the back door. When he opened it, her face was washed with tears.

"My father's going to be here in two days," she said. "He's coming to take me away."

Tut held out his arms before he had time to think. Alex rested her head against his shoulder and cried.

TWENTY-ONE

"HE'S SUPPOSED TO STAY in a motel for a week," Alex said the next morning as she paced in Tut's kitchen. "Gwen says that will give us time to get *acquainted* before she sends me off to Missouri. She doesn't want it to be a shock." Alex shook her head. "You know, she seems so happy about this. It's like her life is going to be so much better once I'm gone. She made me talk to him on the phone last night. I asked him what his favorite food is. You know what he told me? Macaroni. No one's *favorite* food is macaroni.

"He and his wife, Barbra, have a one-bedroom condo. I won't even have my own room. I get to sleep on a couch. He said that Barbra hates the country and doesn't really like the ocean." Alex sighed hard. "He said that my voice reminded him of Gwen's! That is not a compliment."

Tut started to write.

"What are you doing?" Alex asked.

On one piece of paper Tut wrote Alex's name; on another he wrote his. Under her name he wrote *warm sweaters, socks, insulated underwear, raincoat, gloves, books, matches, as many battery-operated things as you can find, food.* Under his name was *water, kerosene, flashlight, food.* As he wrote, he wondered what it was he was forgetting. He knew that there had to be something.

That night Tut was ready. His backpack was in the shed, filled with boxes of macaroni and cheese, a pound of hot dogs, two packages of chocolate bars, and cans of soup. He'd packed as much as he could. Two big jugs of drinking water and a can of kerosene were hidden down by the dock.

Tut had lain awake for hours, waiting for the alarm. Worry had been too powerful to allow him any sleep. It was one o'clock in the morning when he threw back the covers and pulled on every piece of warm clothing he owned. He walked silently past his father's room and downstairs to the kitchen. Alex walked in, looking half awake and miserable.

The harbor was quiet except for the soft lapping sound as the boats rocked gently at their moorings. Alex and Tut stayed close to the edge of the pier until they came to the spot where the skiff was tied. Alex put her backpack into the boat and climbed in quickly. Tut lowered his pack in, then went to the spot where he'd hidden the water and kerosene. He handed them down to Alex. Tut untied the boat and pushed it off as he jumped in. He zipped his jacket higher and pulled the sleeves down over his hands. Cold seemed to come right through the boat and up his legs. He knew it was going to be brutal out past the breakwater. He'd start the motor then.

Alex's back was turned toward him as the boat moved through the channel. The tide was going out and the current helped him. She sat watching the harbor and the few lights that lit the village grow smaller and finally disappear.

"I wonder how long it will take for Gwen to notice I'm gone," she said as she turned and sat facing Tut. "My father should be celebrating by this time tomorrow."

When they pushed out past the barrier, the wind hit hard. Alex pulled sweaters and another jacket out of her backpack. She put on layer after layer and still her teeth chattered. Tut pulled the rope to start the engine; nothing happened. He'd watched his father start it cold a thousand times. Tut adjusted the choke and tried again and again. The fourth time it coughed and the fifth it started. He took hold of the long white handle and turned the end, making the boat move through the night.

"Are there animals on the island?" Alex yelled. She was watching him now. Sitting all hunched up against the cutting wind.

Tut shrugged. There would be birds, maybe a seal once in a while.

"You'll come out every other day?" she asked.

Tut smiled at Alex, realizing that she was afraid. But he knew that he wouldn't like it out there all by himself either.

When they got to the island, the dock had been pulled up for the winter. Tut tied the boat to the stone base. Merrimen was a steep-sided, spruce-covered piece of land, strewn with ancient granite boulders. Tut shone his flashlight up a thin winding path to the camp. There were stone steps up the steepest part. Beside them, bushes grew twisted and close to the ground as if they had been tortured by the wind and salt.

Tut heard a gasp and looked back at Alex. She had gotten her first glance at the camp. It was an old Victorian, covered with red-painted shingles. Porches with heavy wooden arches surrounded it.

Alex's face was pale in the moonlight. Tut took her hand and led her up the rest of the way. At the back door they stopped. There was no sign of a key.

Tut was about to break a window when Alex spotted one. It hung on a nail on the side of the stairs. They unlocked the door and entered the kitchen. Tut shone his light around. The shades were all pulled down. He started looking for the things Alex would need. He tried the faucet. Nothing happened. He was glad he'd brought water. There was an ancient gas stove. He tried one of the burners. The gas had been turned off. Vaguely he was aware of Alex moving off on her own.

"Tut. Look at this," she called from another room.

It was a large room with dark wood trim and deep-green-colored walls. The air was stale and smelled like a thousand old fires. The furniture was draped in sheets. On the walls hung large paintings in bright colors. Tut watched the round circle of her light move over the face of each painting.

"Whoever did these was good," she exclaimed. "Wish Gwen could paint like that."

At the end of a long corridor Alex opened a door. There was a desk with pots of every possible colored pencil, stacks of fresh paper, boxes of pastels, an old green flowerpot with drawing pencils and pens. There were jars of powdered paint and bouquets of brushes. Alex glowed with delight.

"I'll live in this room, Tut! Look at all this stuff!"

Huge windows filled two sides of the room. It would be lovely with the sun pouring in. But now the house was cold and dark and Tut was more concerned about light and heat. In almost every room there was a fireplace, huge, gaping, and impractical for Alex.

He went back to the kitchen. The ancient refrigerator stood empty. In the pantry he found a kerosene heater, a small cookstove, and lamps that he could fill. At least she could have some warmth. The food should last well past his next visit. He went back down to the boat and brought up the water and kerosene.

When he came back, Alex opened a door in the hallway between the living room and kitchen. They pointed their lights up a thin set of stairs. Three bedrooms were up there. While Alex looked around, Tut hunted through closets. He found plenty of old blankets and pillows stored away. They carried them all down to the studio. Alex pulled cushions together in the corner of the room to make a bed.

"Stay with me till I fall asleep?" she asked, a note of pleading in her voice. He couldn't leave her. Tut sat beside Alex on the cushions. She snuggled close to him. He could feel the warmth of her body through the heavy blankets.

"Think of me all the time. If you keep thinking of me, I'll be okay."

He pulled the covers in around her neck and gently brushed her forehead.

"I wish you could stay too," she said.

He watched her eye lids grow heavy. He wanted to kiss her cheek. His mother had done that when he went to bed and it seemed the right thing to do, but he couldn't.

When he was sure Alex was asleep, he crept out of the room, hating the fact that he was leaving her alone. The moon was shining as he walked through the thick woods. Tut untied the boat and pushed off.

He'd have to take his father's leather coat next time. He forced his teeth together till his jaws ached and endured the trip over the deep, black water.

In the harbor Tut tied the skiff to its mooring and ran home. He thought of what Alex had said once: "Normal people are afraid of the dark." From the moment he'd left the island, he'd felt like something was reaching out from the sea to pull him in and he *was* afraid.

TWENTY-TWO

USUALLY THE SCREECHING GULLS woke Tut, but this morning the sound of his alarm jarred him awake. He lay there for a second in the warmth of his bed and it all came back. Alex was no longer on the mainland. The only way that he could know she was all right was if he went to the island.

Tut knew he had to get up that instant or he was going to slip back to sleep. His job, for now, was to make it appear as if nothing was wrong. That job seemed enormous. He wondered how long it would be until Gwen noticed that Alex was gone.

He drank two cups of the strongest coffee he'd ever made and went to school.

"Are we interrupting your nap, Mr. Tuttle?" his second-period math teacher asked.

Tut sat up straight and forced himself to stay awake.

He hadn't slept a bit before they'd headed out to the island and couldn't remember ever being this tired.

There was still so much to think about. They had agreed that he wouldn't go every night. She'd still have plenty of things to eat and drink. If he went out every day, someone would catch on. What should he bring her the next time he went? What would she need?

Alex's empty seat screamed at him during English. It felt like a finger pointing across the room. Miss Berry asked him questions that he couldn't answer because he hadn't been listening. He found that if he sat in precisely the right position, if he leaned back in his chair and tilted his head just enough to balance it on his spine, he could almost sleep sitting up.

"Jamie." Miss Berry's voice came through the haze and Tut woke with a start. "I want to see you after class."

Half an hour later, when the other students walked out, Tut sat waiting.

"Your father told me what the last few years have been like," she started. "I've read your records, of course, but I had no idea you two had been through so much." She walked to the window; her face was silhouetted against the afternoon light. "Your father said that it did him good to talk about it. And that made me wonder, Jamie; you need to express your feelings too." She went to her desk and picked up a notebook. It wasn't much larger than a novel. The cover was black. She handed it to Tut.

"I'm going to give you this. I want you to write everything that comes to you." She looked hard into Tut's face, as if she was trying to read his mind through what she saw in his eyes. "When you write down those painful thoughts, it sometimes helps. It almost frees you from their hold. You seem so far away today. I hope I haven't pushed you too hard. If I have, I'm sorry. But let's try this. Turn it in to me when you feel you're ready to. Okay?"

Tut ran his fingers over the surface of the book. *I don't know where to begin.* He signed the words slowly and then looked up at her.

"Start there. Write down on the first page, 'I don't know where to begin.' It will come."

I hate lying, Tut thought as he walked home alone. *I'm not good at it.* But then he hadn't really had to lie yet. What would happen if Alex's mother asked him questions? Or the police? If he had acted strange today, Miss Berry thought it was because of his life, not because he'd helped Alex run away.

Tut worked for Mr. White after school. The afternoon

was so quiet without Alex's chatter. Later, after he had eaten dinner, he went up to his room and looked out at the island. There was no light. Nothing to show that anyone was there. He fought the urge to get in the boat. He was bone tired and wanted to sleep, but the book lay on his bed and he couldn't ignore it. After staring at a blank page for a while, he started to write.

I would start at the beginning, but I don't know where the beginning is. Did it start the moment she died, or was that the end? It seems more like the end to me. The end not just of my mother's life, but everything. Something stopped then that was so much more than we knew it was before. Yet there was the beginning of something else. Something that has colored and influenced everything since then. When she was alive, we lived constantly in the presence of joy and light and didn't know it until that joy stopped, until that light was gone. I took her so much for granted. It shouldn't have been that easy for her to die.

Tut closed the book, turned off his light, and pulled the blankets up around his neck. He was so tired that he should have gone right to sleep, but as he lay there, he felt the worry of it come. Like something awful was just outside his window, waiting. He rolled onto his side and tried to sleep.

The next morning he expected Gwen to be banging at the door, but she wasn't. It was Alex's theory that it would take days for Gwen to notice that she was gone. Her father should be here by now. Wouldn't they start searching? When he looked up the hill, he could see a strange car, but no sign of the police. Alex said that her mother would call the police only as a last resort.

He was restless all day in school but tried not to show it. He wondered how Alex's supply of water was holding out. What was she doing all day? After dark he'd pack the boat and go to her.

"Tut, I ain't got much fer ya to do today," Mr. White greeted him after school. "Besides, ya look like hell. Why don't you go home and get some sleep? Are you feeling okay?"

Tut stood looking at the old man. He hated to ask for money. If it wasn't for Alex, he'd have just turned and walked out.

Mr. White looked at him as if wondering what he wanted. "Oh, fer cryin' out loud. I owe you fer yesterday, don't I?"

Tut nodded and took the money and stuffed it in his pocket.

"Don't spend it all on that little filly," Mr. White said, and Tut froze. "I been watching you. When a man gets a girlfriend, two things happen: time and money disappear. Ain't had a minute to myself or a dime of my own since I met my wife."

Tut walked through the store, looking and checking prices. With what Mr. White gave him and what he already had, there was fifteen dollars in his pocket. He chose things carefully. A good-sized box of oatmeal, some oranges, a quart of milk, and a bag of Oreos. A jar of peanut butter, half a pound of salami, a box of crackers, a jar of grape jelly, and three candy bars. It came to fifteen dollars and forty-five cents. He found a nickel for change in one pocket, but that was all.

"Don't you worry about that, Tut," Mr. Baker said. "Bring me the forty cents when you can. And if you can't, I won't suffer too much."

Tut went home, packed everything in his backpack, and waited.

The sky was hung with low clouds when Tut crept out of his house after midnight. Every light was on up at Alex's house. The pack was heavy, but still he walked as fast as he could to the harbor. He filled large containers with water outside the market and put them in the boat. Long ago he'd memorized a chart of the night sky. But tonight there wasn't a star visible to guide him.

When he'd rowed past Sutter's Point, he started the engine and headed in what he hoped was the right direction. Knowing if he missed the islands and got in the currents, the small engine would be useless. The sea was covered with long slow swells. There could be a storm coming. Tut had been so busy getting ready that he'd forgotten to listen to the weather station. The swells weren't very high yet and there seemed to be little wind. But the air was bitter cold.

It seemed like he'd gone too far. He was beginning to think that he'd missed it completely when the stony shape of Merrimen came out of the darkness right ahead of him.

When he got out of the boat, Alex tackled him and wrapped her arms around him.

"Oh, it's so good to see you! Better than good! Wait till you see what I've done to the studio, Tut! Just wait till you see it!" She grabbed his hand and started to pull him up the hill.

He stopped her. He pulled on her arm. In the dark shadows she stepped close to him.

"What?" she asked, suddenly quiet and worried. "What is it?"

Tut wanted to look at her face, just study it in the flashlight's beam. Tut pointed to the boat.

"You're wonderful," she cried, and kissed him quickly on the cheek. Tut handed her the backpack, then grabbed the two jugs. They staggered into the kitchen and she started rummaging through the bag.

"Oreos!" she squealed. "Milk, did you bring fresh milk?"

Tut pointed to the backpack. Alex pulled out the carton, opened it, and took a long drink. She stuffed more cookies in her mouth.

"You didn't steal this stuff, did you?"

He shook his head and smiled as she found the Snickers bars.

Alex grabbed two oranges and headed off toward the studio. "Come on, wait till you see."

The room was lit by candles. They flickered against the draft as the door opened and shut, making soft circles of light dance in the huge room. Tut gasped as he looked around. Alex had drawn on one of the walls. It was a huge mural of his secret beach. The one he'd made her be quiet on. He wondered what the name of the crime was if you broke into a house and drew all over it. There must be some technical name, like "illegal decorating of private property."

Alex looked disappointed. "Don't you like it?" she asked.

Tut nodded slowly. She'd used pastels. The colors were rich and bright. The fire tore through the center of the picture like a living flame.

Tut picked up a piece of charcoal that lay on the table and wrote on a tablet, *It's good, Alex. Really good.*

She smiled and made him sit on the piles of cushions she called a bed.

"Wait till I show you what I found." Alex opened a closet in the far corner of the room. "Look at this stuff," she called as she pulled out costumes of all kinds.

"This is my favorite," she said as she held up a long silver dress with blue and purple veils. A high screen stood at one end of the room and as Tut sat on the cushions, Alex dashed behind it.

"Wait till you see this; it's gorgeous," Alex said from behind the screen. She came out and danced about the room, swirling to make the veils fly out behind her. She danced about to music that he knew was in her head.

"Come, dance with me!" She laughed.

Tut smiled but shook his head. Nope, he wasn't a free spirit who could just dance around the room. He knew himself better than that.

Suddenly the chill of the room got to Alex and she

dove into the cushions beside him and covered up with the blankets. "It's warm in here during the day when the sun beats in. Has Gwen realized that I'm gone yet?"

I haven't heard anything, Tut wrote.

"Figures." Alex just looked at him and shook her head. She pulled a heavy Hudson blanket around her shoulders. Tut got up and went to the kitchen to get kerosene, taking a flashlight to light his way. He filled the heater with fuel, then went to the pantry. He looked over the contents of the small room. There were various pots and pans. As Tut checked through the shelves, something yellow in the far corner caught his eye. He held the light near it. It was a raft. Next to it was a foot pump. He didn't like that. He put them way up on the top shelf, as far away from the edge as he could push them.

TWENTY-THREE

BACK IN THE STUDIO, Tut lit a match and the heater roared, then settled down to a soft hissing. The smell of kerosene was strong.

Tut took a candle and started looking at the bookshelves. There were rows of art books: Van Gogh, Matisse, Winslow Homer, Monet—Tut knew them all. His mother had books about those artists, but there were others he'd never heard of. He held the candle close to the bindings as he read their names. *I'd like to read about them all someday,* he thought.

There was a section of poets too. He read the names: Browning, Tennyson, Byron, Emerson. They were all names that brought images, words to his mind. His eyes rested on a thin volume of poetry. His throat started to hurt.

"What are you looking at, Tut?"

He took the book off the shelf and turned the pages.

"Do you really like old poetry?" Alex asked. Her words asked the question, but the tone of her voice said, "Are you nuts?"

He opened it to a certain page and handed the book to Alex. If she read the words, she'd understand. She got up and went to sit near the heater. She placed a candle on the table and looked up at him with a funny expression.

"The title is awful, Tut. 'Dirge without Music.' Let me guess—this is your favorite poem, right?"

Tut watched her face as she read the words. She closed the volume, turned it around in her hands. Finally she looked at Tut. "Is that how you felt when your mother died?"

Exactly, he wrote.

Alex stood up and twirled slowly around the room, through the pools of candlelight. She collapsed on the cushions beside Tut. He put his arms around her and she rested her head on his shoulder.

"What do you write in those letters, the ones in the bottles?" she asked.

Tut wrote on the piece of paper beside him. *Poems. Sometimes I write about things that happen. Sometimes I just write. Why?*

"You send them to your mother, right?" she asked.

He nodded.

Alex took the two oranges that she'd brought from the kitchen and handed one to Tut. She pushed her thumb into the end of hers. The thick citrus aroma filled the air. She tore the orange apart and put a section in her mouth and chewed.

"Things like that shouldn't happen, Tut," she whispered. "I wish she was still alive." Alex was about to put another piece of orange in her mouth when she looked at Tut. "I know this sounds bizarre, but I think you communicate more with your mother than I do with mine."

She finished her orange, then leaned back against his chest. He pulled the blanket up to cover them both. The wind seemed to be blowing a bit harder now. He shouldn't stay long. It was so late. Just another few minutes with Alex beside him. The scent of her hair was wonderful and he knew she'd been outside pacing the island, waiting for him. He closed his eyes for just a minute. It wasn't long before he was sound asleep. He dreamed of a great wind with an angry voice and waves breaking against stones.

Rain was battering against the windows on the east side of the house when Tut woke. He looked at his watch. It was almost four. The fishing boats would be going out in only an hour. He made sure Alex was covered well, blew out the candles, turned off the heater, and ran to the back door. Rain poured down the glass in thick gray sheets. This wasn't just a normal storm. It was one that had built up power over the ocean and was pounding its fury back against the land.

It was insane to go out in this, absolutely crazy, and Tut knew it. But he had to get the boat back before his father needed it or everyone would know.

Tut cursed himself as he slid down the trail to the boat. He untied it and tried to push off, but the wind blew the boat back into the rocks. Tut leaned over the side and shoved it away, battling his way around the side of the island. Finally he was out in the open sea. His coat was already soaked through. Rain hit his face, feeling more like small, sharp stones. Water sloshed around his feet.

He pulled on the cord to the motor until he thought his arm would fall off. Finally it hiccuped, coughed, and then started. Tut turned the boat and headed for the mainland, riding up and down on the deep swells. He tried to guide the boat toward the channel and not the rocks by Sutter's Point.

He closed his eyes and prayed as the icy wind cut through his wet clothing. As he neared the land, he could hear the breakers roaring. There was usually a different sound when the waves broke on rocks and when they broke on sand. But as he struggled to find something in the night to aim for, all he could hear was a constant deafening roar.

Lights from shore flickered and disappeared. He wasn't really sure where he was. The light at Mosher Point was just barely visible. But it was little help. He couldn't judge how far away it was. The roar of the breakers grew louder. If he hit the beach, he might be okay. If he could find the channel to the harbor, he would be all right. Those were two very tiny spots on a huge coast. In this weather it would be a miracle if he could find either.

The motor sputtered, stalled, and died. Without the motor he had no way of controlling the boat. Tut tried to start it, pulling the cord frantically, but nothing happened.

TWENTY-FOUR

TUT HAD BEEN so careful about details, taken so much time to memorize the stars, and now he was the one in the boat about to die. Tut thought of the fear he had of speaking. He felt that same kind of fear now. Swells rushed over the sides, but Tut had no time to bail. All he could do was hold on.

The boat rose up the side of a huge swell. It crested the top. He held on as tight as he could while the boat swept down the face of another wave. There was a brutal jarring and the horrible sound of wood breaking on stone and Tut was thrown into the cold water. He struggled to the surface only to have another wave force him into the rocks. The second the pressure relaxed, he fought his way up. His face broke the surface and he gasped for air. Almost immediately he was pulled back down, battered against the rocks.

It felt like his lungs would explode. Another gasp of air and another wave, driving him down again. He wrapped his arms around his head to protect it. He was being pushed in toward shore. There was more and more sand between the stones and a shorter distance between the bottom and the surface. He had to get up on the beach, away from the rocks and the waves. The sound was bearing down on top of him and he was slammed again.

Tut felt his right arm snap and he knew it was broken. The next wave hit, it pulled and tore at him, but he didn't try to fight it this time. The pain in his arm was huge and he held the wounded arm to his stomach with his other hand, trying to keep it still so it wouldn't hurt so much. This was it. This was what it felt like. There was a peace about it, a calmness, a surrender.

What about Alex? What would happen if she stayed out there? The raft! That damned yellow raft. One more heave of the waves and he pushed with his legs. Finally he lay in the cold sand, coughing up seawater. He took deep breaths. Another wave hit him and he knew he had to get farther up on the sand or the waves could still drag him out to sea.

The rain kept coming down. He heard the poet's words in his mind. The outrage at death, how final and unacceptable it was. He tried to stand, but the pain in his arm was too much and he just lay still, trying not to move. Darkness and cold were creeping in.

There was a humming sound. Words kept screaming in his ears, but he couldn't understand them. It seemed to Tut that the words were floating above him on the water. He knew he should be fighting his way up to the surface. But he was unable to move.

"Broken arm," he heard someone say. "Hypothermia," he heard in the same voice. Then in answer, "I told you that you needed to spend more time with the boy." Gramma Esta was there and he let himself sink back down.

It was quiet again and dark when he finally made it to the top.

"You're awake?" His father put his hand on Tut's head. "Good Lord!" he said, and left the room. Tut's head pounded and his throat felt scorched. Every joint ached. A nurse stuck a thermometer under his tongue. He tried to ask how long he'd been there, but his arm felt like it was encased in stone. He couldn't move his fingers.

Alex. The yellow raft! He tried to sit up but couldn't.

His father took his shoulders and held him down while the nurse came toward him with a needle. He had to tell them somehow. If he didn't, the current would take the yellow raft away forever.

"What's wrong with him?" he heard his father's voice. "What's wrong with my son?"

The needle penetrated his arm. Tut looked into his father's eyes. All he could see was fear and that turned gray as the surface closed above him again and he floated back into darkness.

"So they don't have any idea where the girl is?" Tut heard his father say.

"No." It was Miss Berry. "The only one who might have any idea is Jamie. They were close. I guess Alex was gone for some time before Gwen realized it. Then with Jamie being like this for five days now? I just hope Alex is all right. Gwen's afraid that she was with Tut in the boat. She's just about crazy with worry."

Tut could feel himself sinking. "Mmmm," he struggled with the word. He could feel the old fear growing. His heart began to beat harder and his breathing was labored. He wanted to sign the words, but his arm was strapped to his chest. He tried to move his left hand. It was taped to an IV.

Tut's father was beside him. "Tut?"

"Mmmm," he moaned as he looked up into his father's burning eyes.

Tut took a deep breath. There was no time to be afraid.

"Mmmer-a," he tried again. Tears streamed down his face. But he had to make them understand.

"He's trying to say something," Miss Berry said.

"What is it?" His father's face was so close now.

"Mmm-er-a-mmm," Tut said.

"Merrimen?" his father said.

Tut nodded. "A-ex." He forced the words out.

"Is Alex on Merrimen Island?" his father asked.

Tut collapsed back down into the pillows. He closed his eyes and tried to quiet his breathing.

His father dialed a number quickly on the bedside phone. "Kramer, this is Winston. Jamie just told me that the missing girl is on Merrimen Island."

Tut struggled again. "Rrrr-ed," said Tut.

"The old red cottage?" he asked Tut.

Tut nodded again.

"Yes, in the old red Victorian. You know the one." There were tears running down his father's cheeks. "No, Kramer, I tell you he *told* me."

"Rrr-af," Tut whispered, and it seemed a bit easier.

"What?" Winston got as close as he could.

"Rrr-af, pa-pantry," Tut whispered.

"Tut says that there's some kind of raft in the pantry.

Must be an inflatable." His father looked at him and Tut nodded. "If she's not on the island, check and see if the raft's gone."

What would Alex have done in five days? Tut wondered. Rain spotted the window near his bed. The wind beat it about. If Alex was in the cottage with the fire going, she'd be fine. If she was in the raft, they'd never find her.

"Kramer will have every boat in the harbor out there if the Coast Guard doesn't find her."

"C-cur-rents," Tut whispered.

He looked into his father's eyes and read them well.

"We'll worry about that when we have to. It's so good to hear your voice again." He ran his hand over Tut's hair. Usually that relaxed him, but Tut felt like screaming. He wanted to be the one to rescue Alex. He wanted to know right now that she was alive.

TWENTY-FIVE

TUT WOKE FROM a savage dream. His father was asleep in one of the chairs. Miss Berry sat reading a magazine. She looked up when Tut stirred.

"A-ex?" Tut whispered.

"Not yet," she said.

His father woke and came to sit beside him. "They didn't find her at the cottage."

Tut closed his eyes. His father took his left hand and held it tight. "The raft was gone. Every fisherman in Maine is out in the water looking for her. If she can be found, they'll find her."

Tut lay in the bed, feeling as helpless as a clam. It wasn't a feeling he liked at all.

At ten a nurse came in. "Well, now that you're taking nourishment we can unhook you from this thing." She very gently pulled out the IV, then checked his blood pressure and temperature. "All normal, Mr. Tuttle. I'll be back to give you a bath in a few minutes."

Tut stared at the ceiling and tried to make some pattern of the dots that peppered the tiles. He felt like he wanted to lie there in the quiet and scream. Where was Alex? What was she doing? Was she okay? His father's foot tapped the floor. Tut knew he felt it too.

"Ta-take me?" Tut asked.

His father was silent for a minute. His mouth formed a straight line. Tut could have sworn his answer would be no.

"If you can stand up without falling over, I'll take you out."

"Are you crazy?" Miss Berry said.

"Yup, I'm afraid it runs in our family. I just know that it's a hell of a lot better to be doing something than sitting around worrying."

Tut sat up and held on to his father's arm. As soon as he could muster the strength, he slipped his feet down on the cold linoleum and stood. He didn't fall. His father had brought fresh clothes and he dressed Tut as if he was a small child. He was gentle but quick and seemed to feel an urgency too.

"I should scream for a doctor," Miss Berry said, as she helped Tut on with his shoes.

"But you won't," his father said.

"What would be the use?"

"None," his father grinned at her, relieved that she was finally catching on.

Sneaking out of the hospital was easier than any of them thought it would be. When they reached the truck Tut fell into the seat. Every part of his body hurt, but he needed to go to that island more than he needed anything else.

Within an hour they were in the *Merry Anna II*, headed out toward Merrimen. The sky had cleared. The sea was calm. Tut marveled at the way the ocean changed. His father's face was paler than he'd ever seen it. He'd changed too, but Tut was afraid to trust it. It would be like trusting the sea.

As they neared the island, he searched every line of stone and tree for a sign of Alex. They dropped anchor in safe water and then rowed a borrowed skiff to shore.

Tut was used to doing things when he hurt. He usually just ignored pain, but this was weakness and his whole body ached. His father helped him out of the boat and practically carried him up the path to the cabin.

They pushed open the door and were met with silence. Tut went slowly through the hallway to the studio.

Outside the door he paused for a moment, afraid to open it. Gently he pushed the door. The shades were all drawn. The pile of cushions gone. The room looked almost as it had when they first saw it. Alex had put everything back. It felt like a tomb.

She'd done more drawing on the walls. In thick black crayon was written, *I'm as bored as bored can be, won't you come and rescue me?*

Tut, where are you? I have read all of your old poets. You haven't been here for three days. I'm thinking way too much.

Who are you, Tut? Did that nickname shut your mouth forever? You were never supposed to be a Tut, silent like a statue, you were supposed to be a James, strong and honest and good.

We finally know who we are when we're alone. I thought I was brave, but I'm not. I thought I was strong, but I'm not that either.

He stumbled through the house, frantically looking in every spot big enough to hide. He had to look upstairs. Tut could feel his father's hands supporting his back.

"Son, I'm sure they've been all over this house."

In the front upstairs bedroom he stopped. The window was open slightly. A breeze made the curtain move into the room. He caught sight of the gray-green water.

"Alex," he whispered.

Tut walked out of the house and through the trees to the highest point of land. An outcropping of stone that stood above a rocky beach. He looked across the endless water to the very edge of the horizon. There was not a speck of yellow.

Would the sea take everyone he loved? Tut watched the waves break on the rocks below him. It was thirty-five, maybe forty feet from where he stood.

"Come back away from the edge, son," his father said.

Tut stood firmly. There was one thing he needed to know before he moved in any direction. He turned his head and looked at his father. His throat hurt so much that he could barely say the words. They came out rough and halting.

"Wa-was it my fa-fault Mom d-ied?"

"Oh God, Tut." His father's face seemed to dissolve, his lips trembled. "It wasn't your fault. It wasn't my fault. It just happened. Sometimes awful things just happen." He walked to Tut and pulled him into his arms. Tut broke into sobs. His father held him tight, so tight that he could feel the strength of his father's arms and the power of his pain.

His father helped Tut down the rocks to the safety of the path. When they were back in the big boat, they turned and headed out toward the open sea.

"I'm following the current," his father yelled above the sound of the motor. "If she went this way, she would have been caught by it. If she'd gone on the other side, they'd have found her already."

They followed the current until it disappeared. Tut couldn't see land, just water, open and clear.

"*Merry Anna II,* this is Kramer. Come in, please." They barely heard the radio above the engine.

"This is the *Merry Anna II,*" his father said into the radio's mike.

"Hey. I've been trying to get ahold of you two. The Coast Guard picked up a girl in a yellow life raft about two hours ago."

TWENTY-SIX

NOVEMBER.

TUT READ THE OLD POETS out loud until he couldn't stand the sound of his own voice anymore. Words came easier now. His strength was slowly coming back. The arm was healing and the bruises on his body were almost gone. A few more days and he'd be back in school. What would it be like, being there and being able to speak? Tut wasn't looking forward to it.

Tut was surprised when Miss Berry came by with his homework assignments. He was hoping that she'd send them through Alex. But Gwen wouldn't let Alex anywhere near Tut. Miss Berry brought a fish casserole and a salad too. After they'd talked about school and the casserole was in the oven warming, she left.

His father came home smelling of the sea and nothing else. "You got a really good teacher," he said, opening the oven door.

"She's nice," Tut said. He was wondering if she brought casseroles with homework assignments to every student.

His father looked at him. "What?" he asked.

"I just said she's nice," Tut answered. "That's all."

The first day he was able to walk to the point, a fog was moving in, looking as if it was rolling the water flat as it came. He didn't hear Alex coming up behind him. She sat down and craned her neck to look into his face.

"Hey!" he greeted her.

"Hey," she said, and smiled. "I heard a rumor that you were talking and I wanted the first word that we shared to be yours."

Tut laughed. "That would be a change, wouldn't it?"

"You sound just like I thought you would."

"I'm glad you're alive," Tut said.

"Me too." She ran her fingers through her hair, combing it back from her face.

"Will you be moving?" Tut didn't want to ask but had to.

"No, not permanently. I'm not really sure what's happening," she said. "Well, I met my dad. He stayed around for a few days after they found me."

"What's he like?"

"He's taller that I thought he'd be. He has my eyes and hair, except less of it. He drives a motorcycle." She took a deep breath. "We talked for hours about all kinds of stuff. He's not a jerk. He just doesn't have a clue how to be a father. He likes poetry and Gwen drives him nuts, so we have some things in common."

"Are you going to Missouri?"

"Just for vacations. Dutch, that's my father's name, he said that he'd like to get to know me. And I guess it wouldn't be a bad thing to have a backup. You know, one sane parent is better than none."

"Gwen hates me," Tut said.

"Oh yeah. She does. But she'll get over it."

"How are things with her?"

"It's funny. Because I ran away, they made us see a counselor. So we've been talking. I guess she really didn't know how she felt about me until she thought I was dead. She was insane when I was out there. I didn't know it would make such a mess for everybody. Are you okay? How's your arm?"

"It's healing," Tut said. He took her hand in his left and held it, warming her fingers with his own.

"How's your dad?" she asked. "Does he hate *me*?"

Tut shook his head. "Naw, he doesn't hate you. Sometimes he's calm and sometimes I can feel him getting all stirred up inside. I don't know how he'll be tomorrow, but he's been different."

"I want you to come with me," Tut's father said early Saturday morning. They'd just eaten breakfast and he was putting the dishes in the sink.

"Where?" Tut asked. He still used words sparingly with most people. The anxiety about talking was gone, but one thing he learned through his years of silence was that people talk way too much.

"I have something I want to show you."

Tut couldn't tell by looking at his father's face what it was. He followed him to the truck and they drove silently through town. A cold, bitter wind blew off the sea, and when the truck stopped and they got out, it hit them hard. Beside the truck was a gate in an old stone wall and beyond that, the cemetery.

Winston Tuttle opened the gate and walked between the stones toward the crown of the hill. Tut followed. A bare-limbed maple stood about ten feet away from a new stone. Tut read the words *Anna Marie Tuttle.*

"I never told you when they found her body." Winston's voice seemed weak in the cold wind. "There was an old man, Mr. Fernier. I don't know if you remember him. He pulled up his line and she was caught in it.

Far as I know, he never fished again. I had to identify her and I don't remember much after that. By the time I came around, they'd put her here. We'd already had the funeral but hadn't found her and didn't know if we ever would. I didn't know how to tell you. Every time I thought of buying a stone, I couldn't stand it. Seemed like seeing her name carved across it would make it too real. I'm sorry for all I haven't done, Tut, and I'm sorry for all that I have too."

Tut stared at his mother's name on the dark granite. It did make it too real.

"That day I went to apologize to Miss Berry, she said that you were a son any man would be proud of and it would be nice if I gave you a father that you could be proud of too. I know that trust gets broken easy and I've beat the hell out of ours, Tut. But I'm trying."

Tut wanted to say it was okay, but it wasn't. It hadn't been easy or good or okay and although Tut had hope, he also had doubts.

"I'm trying too," Tut said.

His father held out his left hand. They clasped hands and both knew the thinness of the threads that held them. But Tut hoped, because of the place where they stood and what they'd been through, that the promise would grow into something real and strong.

"Come on, Tut. Let's go."

Tut didn't move. "I don't want to be called Tut anymore."

His father looked at him. "Jamie?" he asked.

Tut thought of the wall at the camp and the words Alex had written. Tut was the name of silence, and Jamie seemed like the name of a child.

"James," he said. "I want to be called James."

His father nodded and started down the hill while Tut stared at the stone. The edges of the letters were sharp. The surface was without any of the stains that marked the other, weathered stones. All that time and so many words sent into the sea, to a woman who lay under this very soil. Beyond the stones that surrounded him, light sparkled on the bay. At the bottom of the hill his father opened the gate and stepped into the road. He was different, his father. It was as if the last few months had brought him from his own grave back to life. That seemed like a choice they each had to make.

The cold wind bit at Tut's cheeks. Maybe winter wouldn't be so bad this year. There were changes that lay ahead but he had made it through so many already. Besides, change didn't seem to frighten Tut that much anymore.

He looked back to the stone. Her name was just a

fragment of who she really was; the best of her lived in his mind and heart and he knew that. "I'm going to be okay, Mom," he said and waited for an answer that he felt more than heard. His father stood waiting by the truck looking small and alone. James walked down the hill. They climbed into the old pickup and drove home together.